A Bridge Spanning Time

Lanette Depew

The Overmountain Press

JOHNSON CITY, TENNESSEE

This book is a work of fiction. All names, characters, places, and events are either the product of the author's imagination or are used fictitiously. Any resemblance to actual events or persons, living or dead, is entirely coincidental and beyond the intent of either the author or the publisher.

Photos on pages 68 and 71 from *Message from the President of the United States Transmitting a Report of the Secretary of Agriculture in Relation to the Forests, Rivers, and Mountains of the Southern Appalachian Region.* Washington: Government Printing Office, 1902

To Lois Huffman Reeves and Lydia, Priscilla, Leo, and Isaac Depew—my mother and children—who in many ways have helped me shape and mold the characters in this story.

ACKNOWLEDGMENTS

Special thanks to Martha Al-Saadi and Esther Hathaway for their editorial comments on the manuscript, to Rozella Hardin for historical accuracy, and to Jason Weems, my editor, for his tireless efforts polishing the manuscript and helping me keep the story consistent. To my husband and best friend, Michael, for all of his encouragement and hard work scanning photographs and making phone calls, and to the many individuals who have generously given me permission to use the timeless photographs that help bring the history of Elizabethton to life.

TABLE OF CONTENTS

HISTORICAL NOTE

The Doe River Covered Bridge was fashioned together in 1882 to provide the small yet growing town of Elizabethton, Tennessee, with reliable access across the Doe River.

Built by Dr. E. E. Hunter and his construction company, the bridge, designed with a Howe truss, was constructed with oak, chestnut, poplar, and pine and rests on two limestone abutments.

History tells us that the first person to cross the covered bridge was Fanny Atwater. Though the author uses lilacs and an errant hat to usher the young girl of twelve into the unfinished bridge, the actual reason she slipped from her pastor father's side to crawl across is unknown.

The Doe River Covered Bridge, which has endured flooding, changing times, and more than a century, still stands and is in continued use today. Each June in the City of Elizabethton, a festival is held where young and old come and celebrate the "Queen of the Doe."

For more information regarding the Doe River Covered Bridge, Elizabethton, Roan Mountain, and Butler, the reader is encouraged to peruse the works of historians Rozella Hardin, Dan Crowe, and Jennifer Laughlin.

A Moment of Reflection

Spring 1976

The sun was just beginning to rise over the misty mountains and filter into the growing city when Laurel leisurely carried her coffee and a small wooden chest through the front room to a rocking chair on the porch. Her family would soon arrive to help her celebrate her 100th birthday, and, though she looked forward to the event, she wanted some moments to herself before the antics of grandchildren and great-grandchildren occupied her time and attention.

Since the death of her husband, Joseph, her family visited her often, so there was little time to feel lonely. A collage of portraits hanging on the wall just above her Victrola indicated she had been blessed with a large number of children, grandchildren, and great-grandchildren. All but a few of them still lived in the neighborhood. The pictures ranged from old-fashioned tintypes to color photographs, and among them was a small snapshot her daughter Meg had recently given her of a newborn girl bundled in a pink blanket.

Laurel's eyebrows knit together as she tried in vain to remember the infant's name. She was certain Meg had told her the normal baby statistics when she had given her the picture, yet maybe with so many newborns through the years her mind had refused to accept any additional names, weights, and lengths.

Laurel took a sip of her freshly brewed coffee and let her eyes survey her front room, neatly arranged with a collection of knick-knacks and heirlooms. Despite its age, her house was still in wonderful condition; Joseph had made sure of it before he died. Laurel's children had long ago given up trying to persuade her to sell the house and come live with one of them. To lose her home would mean losing her independence, as well as the perfect view of the covered bridge spanning the Doe River.

So, to appease the family's concern, a young college girl from Laurel's church was hired to help clean in exchange for room and board, and the yard was kept up by a neighbor boy eager to earn a few dollars extra each week. With this welcomed assistance Laurel was able to remain in the house that she loved so much.

The branches on the tall and full magnolia trees in her front yard swayed in the gentle spring breeze, and the aroma of the wild mint that had moved into her rose garden drifted to her porch. Laurel's aged face eased into a smile. The covered bridge, affectionately known in the community as the "Queen of the Doe," would open once again today.

An inspection had found it unsafe to cross the year before, and many feared that the bridge would never again be put to use. But several men with their power saws, drills, and hydraulic lifts were hired, and soon the termite-eaten beams were replaced with yellow pine from Georgia. How her father would have marveled at the technology of the day! After several months of waiting for the structure to be lifted up and the salt-treated beams eased into place, the bridge was to reopen on her birthday.

This was her most precious gift.

Laurel placed her empty coffee cup on the small wicker table next to her rocker and lifted the lid on the box that lay in her lap. Inside, carefully wrapped in faded tissue, was an old pencil sketch of the covered bridge that she had drawn when she was a small girl. The silver frame enclosing it had tarnished with time, and the glass

Covered bridge closed for renovation, 1976
(Courtesy the Archives of Appalachia, Pollyanna Creekmore Collection,
East Tennessee State University)

was dull and scratched, yet it seemed that whenever her family visited, the picture was passed around and Laurel was encouraged to unravel the vibrant strands from the tapestry of her life.

A sigh of contentment escaped Laurel's lips as she thought about the many stories that were hers to share—stories that all centered on that old bridge. Why, she could hardly remember what her life was like before it was built, as it too would be celebrating its 100th birthday in just a few short years.

Robins chattered back and forth while preparing their nests for their offspring, and the quiet stillness of the river whispered nearby, but Laurel no longer paid attention. She lifted her cloudy blue eyes from the weathered drawing to her beloved bridge.

Visitors would once again come from miles around to photograph it, to capture a perfect reflection in the water below. Families would feed the ducks that swam beneath its wooden truss, and fireworks would brighten the night sky above its rafters. But as Laurel gazed at

The covered bridge reflected in the Doe (Courtesy Johnny Holder)

the snow-white structure that graced the view from her front porch, she knew that it was more than a curio or even a symbol of fine craftsmanship. Throughout the span of her life, the covered bridge had provided many things—a romantic setting when Joseph had swept her off her feet, a refuge for her young family as they escaped the May Tide, and a faithful link to her growing town, which now stretched across the Doe River.

As Laurel set the picture down near her cup and contemplated getting more coffee, several small children playing near the bridge caught her eye. They were dressed simply, their hair was tousled and their shoes worn, yet the very sight of them caused a flood of memories to wash over her. Treasured memories of a day gone by, when she was just a dreamy, carefree child in a tender stage of life, growing up on the east side of the Doe River.

The Covered Bridge

Spring 1882

The train whistle blew as the young, flaxen-haired girl reluctantly settled herself on the east bank of the swollen river with a sketchbook in her lap. Oh, how she had wanted to go across to the fields today! She had seen a cluster of black-eyed Susans blooming the day before and had wanted to draw them before the men of the town plowed up the land for spring planting. But the Doe River was high, and her mother had said the little footbridge was too dangerous to cross.

For nearly a century, her small agricultural village lay nestled at the base of Lynn Mountain, between the Watauga and Doe rivers. The majestic courthouse that stood on Main Street represented not only the town but also the whole of Carter County, which extended far into the mountains. Several gristmills utilized the force of the rivers, and the livery stable, open market, churches, and hotel met the needs of the community, yet there was a yearning to grow in the hearts of the villagers. New Town, as she had heard many people address the fertile land beyond the overflowing waters, was the home of the train depot and even a few families, but for the most part it remained an open field containing room where the cramped village could expand.

Laurel reached forward and trailed her fingers in the cool water as her brother William came running to her with his schoolbooks swing-

"Old Town" Elizabethton from Lynn Mountain, 1890s
(Courtesy the Archives of Appalachia)

ing behind him. As a second grader quite bored with "book learnin'," William was eager to see the immersed footbridge that had kept the New Town children out of school. Tommy and May, their best friends, lived on the west side of the river and complained about the extra chores they were given when they couldn't cross the little bridge, but William was pretty certain the work would be a lot better than spending a day at school.

"Wanna go wadin'?" he asked, sitting down next to Laurel and throwing his schoolbooks into the damp grass.

"You know Momma wouldn't like that. The river's too dangerous," Laurel replied.

The train blew its whistle again as it came to rest at the depot, and Laurel adjusted her position on the bank so that she could draw the covered bridge, which was still under construction. The days when the river was full had forced the town to recognize the need for a better way to cross the river, because the footbridge was proving to be unreliable. High water was not only a problem for the school children; travelers on incoming trains were also inconvenienced if they were planning to stay in town at the Snyder House Hotel, and the doctor was often unable to complete his rounds.

"All right then, ya wanna just skip rocks?" William asked. "I got the perfect skippin' stone here. I found it up yonder yesterday."

"Okay," Laurel said.

She set her sketchbook aside, and for the next half hour rocks skimmed across the river, denting its surface with ripples. Then the two children heard a commotion on the footbridge.

A businessman carrying a small travel case tried to walk on the little footbridge, which was several inches beneath the surface of the risen river. As he started to cross, he shouted, "I don't care if I do get my feet wet! I got some business to do up Stoney Creek, and I aim to get there today!" Fellow travelers stood on the bank, trying to warn the man about the foolishness of crossing the flooded river. Surely his business, no matter how important, was not worth his life, but the man continued on his trek over the insecure bridge, more determined than ever to cross.

"Ever' time I come to this-here town, I got a problem with the bridge. Well, I tell ya, it ain't gonna stop me now!" the man said crossly, and he swung around to glare at his audience with such force that the bridge upset and plunged him headfirst into the cold water.

Carter County Courthouse (Courtesy Guy Burleson)

For the next few minutes the poor man tried to swim against the current, dragging his waterlogged suitcase, until William was able to help him to safety. His suit was dripping wet and the fancy shoes he wore were caked in mud, but as soon as the man reached the shore, he stomped off in the direction of the livery stable, muttering something about a lousy town that didn't have a proper way across one simple river.

The train announced its departure from the station, and Laurel once again settled herself on the bank with her sketchbook. Couldn't the businessman see that her town was building the covered bridge in an effort to connect the two sides of the river? Oak, pine, chestnut, and poplar trees that had once reached high into the heavens were chosen from the nearby mountains, skidded into the valley by a team of horses, and then transported to the bridge's location, which had been chosen even before the War Between the States. Men armed with broadaxes shaped the oak and pine into beams, and steam-powered sawmills split the poplar into weatherboard, and local carpenters thinned the chestnut into shingles with mallets and froes.

Limestone rocks weighing between 750 and 1000 pounds each were also harvested from the land. They were fitted together as an abutment on each bank, using log levers and mules to place them. Those same mules helped wedge in the beams, which were then fastened to the limestone abutments with spikes and bolts. Vertical wooden frameworks that would help support the weight of buggies and burdened wagons were then woven together, and the town witnessed the construction of the bridge, which slowly spanned the 134 feet across the Doe River.

Laurel opened her sketchbook and drew a young girl sitting on the bank near the covered bridge. For weeks, the carpenters had worked to shelter the truss, protecting its beams and frame from deterioration. And now the dream of the villagers to have a better way to cross the river would soon become a reality, as the final process of laying the shingles was nearing completion.

Logging and skid row
(Courtesy the Archives of Appalachia, Charles C. Tiller Collection)

The train had long been gone, and Laurel could see only a trail of black smoke indicating where it had been as it wound its way up into the mountains. The construction of the bridge meant growth for the small village and convenience for its residents and travelers like the businessman, who could still be heard throwing insults at her town. But as Laurel closed her sketchbook and walked the short distance to her home, she liked to imagine the bridge as her own personal link to the fields beyond.

All Things
Came Into Being

A cool Sunday-morning breeze flowed into Laurel's yard, causing her to shiver as she and her family left for the short walk to church. Carrying her sketchbook and Bible exposed her small fingers, and Laurel wished she had grabbed her gloves on the way out the door.

For as long as Elizabethton had existed, the day set aside for worship was important to the small town. Though the spring weather still held a chill, the waters of the Doe had subsided enough for members from both sides of the river to attend, and the church was brimming when the small family arrived.

"Miss Campbell, I drew some more pictures!" Laurel said dramatically, running up to her Sunday school teacher, who had just stepped from her wagon. "Here's a picture of my cat, and I even drew the new covered bridge."

"Why, Laurel, these are quite lovely!" Miss Campbell said. She took a few minutes to carefully study each picture. "You will make a fine artist someday."

Laurel, quite fond of her teacher, helped Miss Campbell transport Sunday school material to her classroom, then she settled herself on a

Horses and carriage crossing the Doe River
(Courtesy Scotti McCarthy and Mary Harrell-Sesniak)

hard wooden bench with her sketchbook and Bible in her lap. The room, which boasted two small windows and a large wooden door, was crowded with several benches marred from years of use and had a chair in front for the teacher. A large slate board bearing Genesis 1:1 in perfect cursive permanently graced the front wall, and a weathered bookshelf laden with extra Bibles ran along the back wall.

Laurel rubbed her hands together to warm them as her friend May came running into the room, carelessly flinging herself on the bench.

"Laurel, guess what," she said, trying to catch her breath. "We got us some new kittens! The momma cat keeps hidin' 'em in the barn, but I'm gonna look for 'em again today. Wanna come over?"

Laurel listened to her friend talk and wondered what it would be like to live across the river, playing with kittens instead of going to school. "I wonder if Momma will let us have one," she said wistfully. Her own cat, Snowy, was old and ornery, and the family had long ago decided to let him retire in peace.

"The white one's back legs are crippled," said May, "but ya

should see him playin' with the others. He acts like there ain't nothin' wrong with him."

The two girls chatted excitedly. Three older boys sat behind them and started to tease. One of the boys was new to the town. Laurel had seen him only once before, when she was out in the fields with her sketchbook. His name was Joseph, and he had just moved with his family into an old farmhouse on the west side of the river.

"Gotcha some kittens, huh?" asked a tall, lanky, redheaded boy named George. "Tell us where you're hidin' 'em so's we can come and see 'em."

"Yeah!" said Harold, Laurel's neighbor and a faithful tormentor of Snowy.

Joseph placed a work-worn hand on the back of the bench, between the two girls, and leaned forward. "We got us some dogs that would love to meet your cats," he said.

Laurel stood to her feet and shouted, "You just leave May's kittens alone, ya big bullies!"

"Laurel! I'm surprised at you," Miss Campbell said sharply. She had just entered the classroom and now stood nearby, with such a look of disapproval that Laurel felt her face grow red with embarrassment. May burst into tears and the boys snickered.

Miss Campbell brought the class to order and began her carefully prepared lesson about the creation of Adam and Eve's first home. Laurel was soon able to dismiss thoughts of kittens despite the boys, who still poked and jabbed at each other.

Her creative mind composed a beautiful garden overflowing with her favorite flowers—it was quite similar to the meadows, which flourished after a spring rain, beyond the covered bridge. She imagined the daffodils trumpeting the arrival of the season with their burst of bright yellow, the petite violets displaying petals that ranged from deep purple to yellow and white, and the Queen Anne's lace, with its lacy cluster of miniature white flowers encircling a single purple one. She allowed steady caterpillars to nibble on the tender leaves of her fanciful flowers so they could gather strength for their upcoming transformation. She welcomed the quiet hum of industrious bees as they collected nectar and left a trail of pollen, ensuring continuing beauty.

"All things came into being by God," her teacher emphasized at the end of the lesson.

Laurel gazed out a window at the fields across the Doe River and marveled at how God could be so big and make such delicate flowers and scatter them right in her own backyard. Surely, Adam and Eve's garden could not have looked more beautiful than a Tennessee field on a spring day.

Back home, the aroma of roast chicken filled the house. Laurel poured ice-cold water into each glass on the large dining room table and then stood back to admire her work. A vase full of daffodils she had picked on her way home from church graced the lacy white tablecloth and the place settings that surrounded it, and Laurel knew her mother would be pleased. She set the water pitcher on the table and went to help carry serving bowls from the kitchen.

Doe River and "Old Town" Elizabethton (Courtesy Guy Burleson)

Meals in the small household were bountiful, and they nearly always included food from her grandfather's farm on Roan Mountain. Laurel's oldest brother, Thomas, worked there, and part of his pay consisted of chicken, pork, and beef, which he brought down to his family following butchering time. During harvest season, Laurel and William also spent time in the cool mountains with their grandfather, gathering wheat and hay from the fields. On these visits they worked from sunrise to sunset and returned with wagons burdened with grain for bread and hay for their horse and milk cow.

When the food was served and all were seated around the grand table, Laurel's father offered up his gratitude for the meal and then encouraged discussion amongst his children. On this particular Sunday, the conversation centered on the covered bridge and the growth of the small town.

"When the bridge is finished, the town will spill over into the fields," he said, and Laurel detected a glimmer of excitement in his voice. "I heard folks talkin' at the mill yesterday about buildin' houses and shops of all sorts. I don't doubt they tell the truth. If the town is meant to grow, the fields offer the perfect place."

"But, Daddy, if the town moves into the fields, where will my flowers go?" Laurel asked when she realized that maybe the completion of the bridge wasn't the good news she had previously thought it was.

"Oh, don't ya fret about your flowers," her father replied. "This town's not gonna grow up overnight. Things take time, and I'm sure they'll be just fine."

Her confidence restored, Laurel spent the remainder of the meal listening to the gentle voices of her father and mother as they discussed the town and the impact of the bridge on its development.

When the dinner dishes had been washed and dried, Laurel and William were given permission to cross the small footbridge to choose a kitten from the litter at May's farm. As they approached the gate, May and Tommy came out to greet them and showed them the best way into the hay barn. The climb up into the rafters took some doing for a girl with so many skirts to maneuver around, but Laurel made it to the loft. William and Tommy had no such hindrances, so they found the kittens first.

"This is the second time the momma cat has moved these kittens today. Those bullies will never find 'em." May said and gave a relieved laugh. They crawled between the bales of hay to find the calico cat and seven contented kittens sleeping at her side. Four of the kittens looked identical to the mother, two were black twins, and the seventh was a small white kitten whose hind legs were twisted underneath him.

"Oh, how cute," Laurel said, gently stroking the imperfect kitten. "It's sad his legs are hurt."

"I don't think they bother him, they just seem useless," said Tommy.

The kitten opened its sleepy eyes, looked up at the child petting him, and stretched his jaws into an enormous yawn. This single act offset his balance, and he toppled over onto his slumbering siblings and surprised mother. In disgust, the mother cat sauntered off, and the drowsy kittens called after her until the children were able to entice them to play with hair ribbons and bits of straw.

"All of the kittens have homes except him," said May, indicating the handicapped kitten, which was happily batting at a swishing tail.

"Then I guess he gets to come home with us when he's ready to leave his momma," said William.

Laurel carefully lifted the kitten and set him down with his playing siblings, and the children marveled at how he was able to keep up with the others by using his front claws to pull his body through the straw.

When the mother cat casually strolled in, calling to her offspring with a deep purr, Tommy and William ran off in search of adventure, while May and Laurel watched the kittens nuzzle into position to nurse.

"Papa said that the bridge should be finished soon," May told

Laurel, who brushed the hay from her skirt and picked up her sketchbook.

"I know," replied Laurel. "Y'all will have to go to school even on flood days."

May gave a wry look and then crawled through the hay to the ladder. In the stillness of the barn, Laurel could hear the distant howl of hound dogs and vaguely wondered if they belonged to the new boy. Her little kitten, with its deformed hind legs, would be defenseless against such fast dogs designed for hunting.

"Good-bye, little kitten," she whispered, caressing his silky fur before following her friend through the hay. "You stay up here with your momma, and soon I'll come get ya and take ya home with me." She descended the wooden ladder, grateful for the protective mother cat and the safety of the hayloft.

Before Laurel crossed the footbridge back over the river, she sat for a while in the tall grass, sketchbook in her lap, finally able to add the black-eyed Susans to her collection of drawings. From her position, she could admire the vast fields, ancient trees, and the covered bridge that stretched across the lazy river. Any day now, her father had said, and the bridge that she had been waiting so long for would be open. Laurel shaded the tip of a flower petal with the side of her pencil, then closed her book and laid her head back onto the soft earth. The whole community had eagerly anticipated the bridge's completion, and yet, because she felt she had been the most eager, Laurel lay dreamily yearning for the day when perhaps she might be the first to cross it.

Laurel and Lilacs

Birthdays at Laurel's house were a cause for celebration, a chance for relatives to visit and saturate the birthday child with their rich Scotch-Irish heritage and Celtic music. The tunes her father, uncles, and grandfather played on violins, pennywhistles, and dulcimers ranged from lively to humorous, and centuries of stories passed down through the family and into the hearts of the children were sung and danced to.

Gifts given to Laurel on her birthday were simple yet priceless. Besides the small handicapped kitten, which had been decorated with a red ribbon and carefully tucked into a basket, she received a new sketchbook and charcoal pencil from her parents and a penny-whistle from her uncle. These gifts were nice and Laurel appreciated them, but the most cherished gift she eagerly accepted that day was a new song her grandfather had written just for her. The traditional birthday tune was either an upbeat limerick hammered away on his dulcimer or a gently plucked lullaby that produced a special effect which outlasted many a gift.

"Your grandmother always loved to stroll among the mountain laurel just after it bloomed into a lovely shade of pink," he said. He began to strum a quiet tune as Laurel positioned herself at his side with the kitten in her lap.

"She would take a knife and gather branches to bring home," he continued. "Then she would hang some of them on the back porch to dry and would trim the rest to fit in that old vase. The laurel brightened up the dinin' room table, but we used to tease her about bringin' in trees from the woods." At this he stopped and smiled at the bittersweet memory of his small wife carefully arranging the flowers into the intricately painted vase she had brought from Scotland.

Laurel remembered her grandmother as a frail sick woman who spent most of her time either stitching away on something or ill in bed. Laurel's grandfather had ensured that the vase he had mentioned remained full of the beloved laurel and at her bedside until her death. Thus Laurel was very familiar with the pink clusters of delicate flowers framed by large, glossy leaves.

She was also sure she knew the path her grandmother had walked. During the summer, when she and her brother played whoopie-hide along the creek, she always hid in the laurel, where she could enjoy its soft fragrance. They had even whittled simple objects from its

Mountain laurel (Courtesy Emma Craib)

straight wood when they tired of their game, and they had tied the sturdy green leaves together to make fans.

"I can still remember the shine in her eyes as she held ya for the first time and whispered your name," her grandfather continued, and a tiny tear trickled down his weathered cheek as he began to sing Laurel's birthday tune:

> *Just as the gentle winds hum on the Roan,*
> *Just as the wild laurel grow,*
> *Whenever I look into your precious life,*
> *I see how His wondrous love flows.*

> *Can you hear how the gentle winds hum on the Roan?*
> *To its tune does the wild laurel sway?*
> *Listen to the music that the mountain brings,*
> *Enjoy it for all of your days.*

> *Just as the wild laurel sways on the Roan,*
> *To the tune of the gentle breeze*
> *When I hear the music of your precious life*
> *The melody's clear and sweet.*

The room was quiet as Laurel hugged her grandfather and thanked him for his gift. Laurel's mother had told her about how she and her grandmother had chosen to name her for the flowers on the mountain, and now the new song etched itself on her heart, just as the flower had long ago.

Following a time of worship and praise to the Creator of music, the handcrafted instruments were laid aside, and Laurel placed the sleeping kitten back into his basket and headed toward the covered bridge to draw. Earlier in the week, she had seen some lilacs growing along the stone abutments, so she decided they would be the first illustrations in her new sketchbook.

The sun was painting the sky with reds and purples as the towns-folk waved from the comfort of their front porches to the small girl walking down the street. Work for the day had been completed and machinery quieted, so they could relax and enjoy "sittin' a spell" while listening to the soothing murmur of the river as it flowed by their growing town.

Laurel chose a spot near the edge of the river and began to sketch the lilacs at the opening of the nearly completed bridge. With only a few remaining shingles waiting to be placed, signs that read NO TROTTING had already been hung at the entrance, and Laurel liked to imagine running across to the fields beyond.

Just as she decided to include a large bumblebee collecting his daily ration of nectar in her drawing, Laurel heard soft voices and turned to see her pastor and his daughter walking toward the bridge.

"The lilacs are just beautiful, Father," the young girl said, inhaling the sweet aroma. "May I pick some to take home?"

Laurel had always liked her pastor, who had nurtured the community while it suffered through the Civil War. His edifying sermons kept even the younger children interested, and he helped rebuild the small church by word and deed. Laurel even appreciated the sentiment that his daughter shared with her about the fragrant flowers, but she secretly hoped he would try to discourage her. To pick some of the lilacs would ruin her drawing, she was sure.

Lilacs

But the preacher, who quietly surveyed the progress of the bridge, nodded his consent, and the young girl began gathering a rather large bouquet until a sudden gust of wind stole her hat and sailed it off into the bridge.

"My hat!" she cried, then giggled as she crawled into the unfinished bridge to retrieve it.

This incident, small though it was, rendered a tremendous sorrow in young Laurel, who still sat with pencil in hand. Oh, how she had wanted to be the first to step onto the new covered bridge. How she had dreamed of skipping across to celebrate her joy of being able to go to the fields even when the waters were high. Now these dreams were shattered as the preacher's daughter, laden with lilacs and wearing the errant hat, walked toward Main Street with her father. A single tear trickled down Laurel's cheek as she felt a keen disappointment she couldn't describe.

Run Through the Mill

The bridge did open the next week, but Laurel had not been able to rekindle the joy she had once felt. While the townsfolk eagerly drove their teams of wide-eyed horses over the flowing river, she chose to watch from a distance. And when the day came for her to collect beeswax from a New Town farm, she did the old-fashioned thing and pulled her little cart over the worn and forgotten footbridge.

"From the look of all of this wax, I do believe we'll have plenty of candles this month," Laurel's mother said as she melted a mixture of sweet-smelling beeswax and tallow harvested from her grandfather's farm. "We may even have enough left over to barter with at the store."

Laurel stood at the large cookstove and quietly began to prime the wicking she had braided earlier in the week, by dipping it down into the hot wax and then holding it up for her mother to pull straight. She was normally fond of candle-making day, even though most girls her age found the job tedious and boring. Laurel had learned long ago that the time she shared making candles with her mother was special. But today Laurel was not in a pleasant mood, and she worked in silence while William chatted with their mother and entertained Jenny, their younger sister, in the corner.

"Pa said I could hitch the team up to the wagon and deliver the candles to the station," William said. "I sure hope the horses don't mind the new bridge." He watched Laurel remove the hardened candles from a special rack where they had rested for several minutes before she rolled them smooth on the polished countertop. "You should have seen ole man Joe's horse when he led him into that bridge. He looked down into the swirlin' waters below, and his eyes got so big I thought for sure he was gonna back out."

Laurel's mother laughed as she sliced the cone off the end of each candle with a sharp knife. She gave the candles a few final dips in the hot wax before handing them back over to Laurel to wrap securely.

"The bridge will be such a blessing," she said. "I'm hopin' the older folks over in New Town will be able to attend church again. Won't that be nice?"

Laurel nodded in response and even offered a polite smile. Her mother was right—the bridge would be beneficial to the small community as it fulfilled its plans to extend across the Doe River. Yet, the truth of the matter is that, while she packed the golden tapers for their long trip by train and wagon to her aunt's shop in Cranberry, North Carolina, Laurel was thinking not about the town or the pastor and his congregation but of the pastor's daughter. How would she be able to face the young girl on Sunday with the secret resentment she held in her heart?

But Laurel did not need to wait until Sunday. The opportunity to confront her newly acquired bitterness came the very next day, when she followed the small country road that led up the river to her father's mill.

The stillness of the wooded area was broken by the rush of the river, which flowed down the man-made raceway and over the large wooden waterwheel at the mill. Inside, the busy hum of wooden gears kept a steady beat, laboring to grind the grain brought by area farmers into smooth, fine flour.

"There she is," her father said, greeting her with a smile as he

Grist mill (Courtesy Brenda C. Calloway)

positioned himself in the grinding area with a large bag of grain. "You're just in time to sweep up this mess I'm gettin' ready to make."

An old farmer stood at her father's side, and the two resumed their neighborly visit while he ground the grain according to the man's wishes. Her father was known in the area as an honest, neighborly man who frequently invited his customers in to visit and view the transformation of their grain into flour.

Laurel's eyes traced the path of the wheat as it was poured into the hopper and then gently tapped down between two millstones powered by the waterwheel and the river's current. The stones had fine cuts, or furrows, that would rip off the outer shell and grind the grain, then direct it out to the edge, where it would slide through a single hole down into a sack.

While her father helped the farmer load the sacks of flour into his wagon, Laurel moved from the entrance of the mill and began counting the burlap sacks of sifted flour received that day in payment. The mill had been a part of her father's life since he was a boy. As an apprentice of an uncle, he had inherited and maintained the thriving business with the desire of passing it on to his own sons.

The interior of the building was whitewashed yearly, which made it look clean and neat despite the dust from the grinding process. The small enclosed office, which contained receipts of past transactions as well as detailed ledgers regarding the upkeep of the mill, was also kept in orderly condition. The river was often cleared of debris upstream to protect the waterwheel and its maze of gears, which were kept in working order with an ample supply of tallow.

Laurel's father employed a number of hired hands and quite often took on apprentices from area farms. Yet, despite the extra help, he preferred to adjust and maintain the heavy stones himself, since a single spark triggered by friction could ignite the freshly ground powder and burn the precious mill to the ground.

"Hello, Preacher! What can I do for ya today?" Laurel heard her father ask when, to her dismay, the preacher and his daughter drove up in a nice yet simple buggy.

"Well, I need some feed for the horse, and my wife sent some eggs in exchange for flour to make bread," the pastor replied as he helped his daughter from the buggy seat.

Laurel retrieved the eggs the preacher's daughter held out to her and carried them to the counter, where she arranged them carefully in the folds of the linen napkin in her mother's basket. She had always liked the friendly pastor, who now discussed the opening of the covered bridge with her father. And as far as the pastor's daughter was concerned, she had always liked her, too. But as the girl stood silently by her father, listening to the two men talk, Laurel could not shake the tinge of anger she stubbornly held on to.

"We just took our first ride over the bridge and visited a few elderly members this afternoon," the pastor said while he paid for the feed. "They were quite excited that we came and said they would be with us to worship from now on."

Laurel's father handed him the small bag of flour, then carried the sack of feed outside and nestled it underneath the buggy seat. "I hear that some of them have been hitchin' up their teams just to take practice runs through the bridge," he said with a quiet chuckle. "They want to be sure the horses are ready come Sunday."

The preacher seemed pleased at this as he helped his daughter into the buggy before climbing up himself and leading their mare away.

When they left, Laurel dangled the small basket of eggs from her arm and walked home along the worn path. As much as she tried, she was not able to keep the pastor's words from her mind. Many of the older folk who lived on the west side of the river had long ago stopped attending the church, fearing the small footbridge wasn't secure. Yet rain or shine, the pastor had visited them and extended invitations.

The covered bridge gleamed in the late afternoon sunlight when Laurel reached town, and the brisk pace she had been keeping suddenly slowed. This bridge she so selfishly coveted was nothing to the pastor's daughter except another way for her and her father to minister to the needs of the people beyond. Laurel began to feel shame for the feelings she had been harboring.

House and road along the Doe River, 1890s
(Courtesy the Archives of Appalachia)

The fragrant aroma of freshly cut wood filled Laurel's senses as she paused at the entrance of the bridge and peered in. The wooden rafters crisscrossing above already manifested life, and baby birds called to their mothers from the safety of their nests. The fine smooth walls reflected the shimmering waters that glistened through the cracks between the wide floorboards. A sturdy rail extended to the far end of the darkened tunnel, reaching to the fields of flowers that beckoned from beyond.

Laurel had not intended to linger, yet as a hay wagon slowly made its way through the bridge, she stepped in and grasped the railing to steady herself. The horse that pulled the precious load seemed sure enough while its heavy hooves thundered across the floorboards, but as it passed, Laurel could see that the horse did not like the idea of walking over the flowing waters.

When the wagon had gone, a warm breeze flowed through the bridge, effortlessly playing with the hay that now lay scattered about, and Laurel felt her inner conflict drain away. The bridge she had anticipated for so long had never been intended to fulfill the whims of a silly girl. It had been built to provide an invaluable service to the community. And as Laurel released her hold on the railing and slowly walked across its wooden truss, she realized how thankful she was that it could also faithfully connect her to the fields of flowers beyond.

The Daisy Chain

Summer 1887

"Hey, Laurel, wait up!"

Laurel slowed her steps to accommodate Jenny, and together they stepped into the covered bridge, which was now five years old.

It had been a hot summer, almost unbearable, and Laurel would have tarried as they walked through the cool shade of the bridge had their errand not been so important. She reached into her apron pocket and felt the small packet of order forms she needed to tuck into one of the crates William had delivered to the train depot the day before. The train now ran all the way into Cranberry, North Carolina, so Laurel and her mother decided to add orders of preserves and sacks of flour to the shipment of candles.

Summer vacation had not really been a vacation at all. The dismissal of school meant more helping hands maintaining the household, which was quite a task. Jenny had taken on Laurel's old chores of caring for the pets, carrying water, and setting the table, so Laurel spent her time in the large garden, tilling, planting, and sowing row after row of vegetables that would feed the family during the mild Tennessee winters. William was also quite busy working as an apprentice at their father's mill along with another boy from school.

When the two girls neared the center of the bridge, they could hear the sounds of snickering from above. Without looking up, Laurel knew that several boys were there, waiting to pounce on unsuspecting pedestrians who crossed over the river. The antics of these boys were well-known throughout the otherwise peaceful community and usually centered on the bridge.

Before Jenny could nervously grab her arm to hasten her onward, Laurel cast a quick glance up into the grinning faces and was surprised that Joseph, who had so long ago threatened the very lives of May's kittens, was not among them. She was sure he could be just as annoying as the rest of them. She had watched him in Sunday school, and though he seemed to be bright when it came time for a catechism drill, he laughed and played with the other boys throughout the Bible lesson.

When they left the bridge and walked along the dirt road to the train depot, May caught up with them, brimming with the latest news and gossip concerning the young people in the small community. Even though she lived on a farm, May possessed a carefree attitude, filling her days with the social activities and happenings in the town.

Laurel had long ago noticed that the dark-haired girl hardly car-

Doe River (Courtesy Guy Burleson)

ried any of the weight at home and that the idle time gave her a wagging tongue. May, on the other hand, felt that Laurel, with all of her duties at home, had little time to keep up with the pastimes of their peers and needed to be enlightened. To Laurel her chattering seemed endless, and quite often she politely listened without really making the effort required for comprehension.

"I was just with Sarah and the other girls, and they told me about a new way to catch a beau," May said.

This simple statement caught Laurel's attention, and she found herself wondering why eleven-year-olds, with several years to come before courting, would waste their time trying to "catch a beau."

"They call it a daisy chain," May continued. "All ya do is link the daisies together, hook 'em across the opening of the bridge, and hide. The first boy to break through the chain will be your beau. It's the fashion. All the girls are doing it."

At the time Laurel had looked at May in disbelief. *How childish*, she had thought, *to think a girl could plan her life in such a trivial way.* But that evening there she was, sitting to the right of the bridge in a rare moment of freedom from her responsibilities, with a chain of black-eyed Susans in her lap. She knew she was being silly, but to gain a glimpse into her own future seemed somewhat exciting. She hoped that some handsome young man would stride into the bridge, right through her chain. Perhaps even plant a small kiss on her cheek to cement the promise.

The chain of the bright yellow flowers with the dark brown centers grew longer as the sun sank lower, and Laurel felt a sudden tinge of nervousness. If she didn't hang it up soon she might lose her chance, because her sister would be sent to fetch her home. The thought of Jenny laughing at her frivolous behavior caused her fingers to loop the green stems together at a brisk pace until she had used each one.

Laurel stood up and held the chain high so she could see how long it was.

"That should do it," she whispered to the miniature sunflowers she had chosen as a lovely substitute for the commonplace daisies. She felt along the bridge's frame and was only mildly surprised at the nails that had been pounded into the wood at waist height. She linked the end of her chain onto a nail, but it was too short to reach across the entrance of the bridge. How could she have been so careless? She had drawn pencil sketches of the bridge at least a dozen times, yet she had no idea how wide it actually was.

The sun was kissing the sky good-night and dusk had begun to settle, so without unfastening the chain, Laurel laid it just inside the bridge and went off in search of more flowers. Because of the late hour, she was content to find daisies, and she didn't make the long hike down the river to the cluster of black-eyed Susans she had harvested from earlier.

When she came back to the bridge with her freshly picked daisies, she heard a loud bit of laughter. To her dismay there lay her precious chain, in pieces, strewn throughout the bridge. A rush of

Daisy chain at the entrance of the covered bridge

embarrassment flooded her cheeks when Joseph suddenly stepped out of the shadows, displaying a cluster of yellow petals in the palm of his hand.

"Waitin' for someone?" he asked. His eyes danced merrily, as if he thought the whole incident a joke.

"How could you?!" There was a tone of iciness in Laurel's voice as she tried to choke back tears. She, who had originally thought the whole craze such a foolish idea, had been caught. Oh, the shame of it all!

She rushed past the grinning boy and down to the path by the river, where she tossed in the remaining flowers. One by one the daisies floated down the course of the Doe, on their way to the Watauga River, while Laurel quickly ran to the refuge of her home. Had she even paused for an instant to look back, she would have noticed Joseph carefully tucking the bright yellow petals into his pocket.

The final days of summer were especially difficult for Laurel. The humiliation of the daisy-chain incident dampened her spirit. Even her love for flowers was squelched; she was sure Joseph had told all her friends about her childish behavior. She feared they would tease if she picked even a single flower. The fact that Joseph had been the other apprentice her father had taken on filled Laurel with little joy when she made trips to the mill to help fill the orders that flooded in from North Carolina.

But soon the weather cooled, as did her cheeks. The fields across the bridge thickened with their flaxen flowers, and Laurel obeyed the intense tug on her heart to lay aside her silly past and explore the jungles of goldenrod and clover, careful to avoid the humbling black-eyed Susans.

A Journey
Into the Mountains

Summer 1893

A refreshing summer breeze blew through the gorge as Laurel supervised the carefully planned activities of the first Sunday school picnic of the year. She and the other young adults in the church had spent several weeks preparing the children's games for the gathering in the Doe River Gorge, and Laurel felt that overall it was a success. She was especially proud of her students—despite the excitement brought about by the train ride, they had behaved quite well, impressing even the older members of the church.

Laurel laughed as she watched her youngest student, Sammy, running toward first base, still carrying the makeshift bat in his chubby hand. She would always be glad she had taken the class when Miss Campbell resigned the year before. With all the preparation and study for each lesson, she felt she might have learned even more than her students had.

But today's lesson had been the last, because she was leaving in the morning to fill the position as governess of a New England family while they vacationed in the majestic Cloudland Hotel at the top of

Train in the Doe River Gorge
(From *A History of Railroading in Western North Carolina,* by Cary Franklin
Poole. Johnson City, Tenn.: The Overmountain Press. Photo by R. F.
Harding, in collection of C. K. Marsh, Jr.)

Roan Mountain. The employment held promise; Laurel would be
responsible for only two children, yet she would miss her students.

The train ride back to town was much quieter. The exhausted
group of children settled down into their seats, and Laurel was able
to mentally plan her route for delivering them to their homes. William
had promised to bring the wagon from the mill to help her, so the task
would not take long.

Laurel's eyes scanned the seats around her and took in the face
of each child. She'd had her times of trial in the past year, yet every
child was dear in his or her own special way. Carrie always had a hug
and a fistful of flowers each Sunday morning, while Jimmy had a
pocketful of treasures. It didn't take too many Sundays for Laurel
to realize class went much more smoothly when she allowed Jimmy to
play show-and-tell prior to the lesson. Peter was shy and quiet and
rarely spoke up in class, and Sammy was bright and eager.

The community's newest batch of rogues proved to be a constant
test to the young teacher. Their antics included frogs, mud, and

even poison ivy, bringing her to her wit's end, until Thomas, father to her three nephews, gave her a few tips on how to handle the boys.

Laurel was surprised to see her father's wagon already waiting at the depot when the train arrived. William had never been that prompt. It wasn't long before the mystery was solved, however, as Joseph stepped out of the depot and headed her way.

"William couldn't come to meet ya, so your father sent me," he said. "Hope you're not too disappointed."

Laurel gave a quick command, and the children formed a line running from youngest to oldest as she took count.

"I don't guess it matters much," she said, "just as long as we get these kids home."

They delivered the children to the farms on the west side of the river first, and Joseph waited patiently while Laurel said good-bye to each child. Her hugs were long and affectionate; she knew the next time she saw them they would be much too grown up to bother with a former Sunday school teacher.

As they headed toward the river and the covered bridge spanning it, Laurel gazed from the wagon to the fields filled with the purple hues of thistle and the creamy white Queen Anne's lace. At dinner the night before, her father had mentioned that some of the leaders were making plans for the new section of town, and Laurel wondered if her fields would boast an extension when she returned.

The old wagon swayed as the mill horse hesitated before allowing himself to be led into the dark opening of the bridge. Up until now, Laurel hadn't realized the embarrassing situation she had allowed herself to get into. The daisy chain incident of so long ago had not been mentioned to any of her friends, and she now found herself fervently praying that it had been forgotten. As they neared the end of the bridge, she pretended to busy herself with the youngsters, but even with the lively chatter of the children she could hear a low chuckle come from Joseph.

* * *

That night, Laurel sank down into the comfort of her bed of feathers, feeling the exhaustion of an emotional day sweep over her. Her mother had helped pack her trunk with several warm dresses, and Jenny carefully wrapped her artist's kit and tucked it between the folds of Laurel's coat. When they were finished, William and her father loaded the large trunk onto the wagon ready to deliver it to the station in the morning.

Saying good-bye to her students had been difficult, but it was the farewells to her family that Laurel dreaded most. Through the years of working side by side each day, she and her mother had developed a bond that went far beyond parent and child, and her father always seemed a source of strength, even in Laurel's most distressing situations. Jenny had proven to be quite a confidante as Laurel still felt the outspoken May unreliable, and William had been a helper in the many chores of the homestead as well as a playmate. Yes, Laurel was sure to miss her family quite a bit.

The next morning, the sun had already warmed the earth by the time Laurel situated herself on a seat in the passenger car and placed a small lunch satchel at her side. Her tears flowed freely while she watched her father finalize travel plans with the conductor, yet the thrill of travel quickened her emotions, making the moment bittersweet.

Laurel gave one final wave to her family beneath the window, then settled back into her seat as steam poured forth from the engine. She and her brother had traveled up the Roan on her grandfather's wagon several times, and she had ridden into the Doe River Gorge by rail for a few Sunday school picnics. But no matter how she had imagined the trip up the mountain would be, she could not have prepared herself for it.

The breathtaking magnificence of the mountains was amplified by the fast pace of the locomotive, which reached speeds up to 30 miles-per-hour on its narrow-gauge track, drawing its passengers and cargo along. The tracks ushered them into the gorge, with its steep sandstone cliffs and cool tunnels, and over bridges a hundred feet above the river. They meandered in and out amongst the mighty hills, often running alongside the Doe River as it cascaded from its birthplace high in the mountains to the valleys below, and Laurel found herself totally captivated by the mountains' splendor.

In the heart of the mountains was a train with a heart. Laurel soon noticed that the train often paused at flag stations to deliver goods the mountain folk had requested from the engineer on his trip into the city. Laurel watched from her window as these deliveries ranged from lanterns and coffee to thread and snuff. But it seemed that parcels from the city weren't the extent of the engineer's generosity. Several young men were given free seats as they dared journey into the neighboring state to court a Carolina girl. Children were given rides home from school, and at one point Laurel watched a farmer hand over a crate of kittens for the engineer to get rid of down the line.

When the train came to rest at the highest point its rails could

Roan Mountain, Tennessee, 1880s
(Courtesy Jennifer Bauer Laughlin, from *Roan Mountain: A Passage of Time*, Johnson City, Tenn.: The Overmountain Press, 1999)

reach, Laurel admired the little town of Roan Mountain, which had grown to accommodate tourists and the railroad. Several shops, a post office, and a hotel adorned the streets, and Laurel could hear the whispering Doe River as she stepped from the train. Here, in this small mountain town, she would stay until morning, when a hack would transport her and the other passengers the remaining twelve miles to the grand Cloudland Hotel.

That evening, Laurel began to write in her travel journal, desperately trying to describe every detail of the thrilling trip up the mountain and the difference in temperature compared to the summer heat in the lowlands. As she expected, her meticulous employer, Mrs. Sanders, had put everything in order, and Laurel was given a delicious meal and comfortable room. But this was her first night away from her family, and a sudden wave of loneliness washed over her as she set the small book aside and questioned the wisdom of leaving the only life she knew.

A Summer
in the Clouds

Early the next morning, the passengers awakened to a dripping sky. They met together at the livery stable and were disappointed to see that the mountain they planned to climb was encompassed by heavy clouds.

"Find yourselves a seat," the driver said. He handed each of them a lunch and packed their luggage onto the back of the wagon.

Laurel climbed up into the wagon, next to a photographer, who packed his precious plate camera under his seat. She had ridden on rough mountain roads several times in the past on her way to her grandfather's house, and she knew comfort was not a part of the fare purchased for her.

As the wagon effortlessly bounced its passengers around, a lady with a fancy overcoat and feathered hat began to complain. "The weather is awfully sour," she said. "Shouldn't we wait until tomorrow?"

The driver removed his hat and let his eyes sweep the trail, which disappeared into a cloud of mist. "Naw, I've traveled this-here road in worse weather than this," he said, skillfully leading the horses.

Despite the drizzling rain and the irritable woman, the trip was tolerable. The driver kept company with the travelers, telling them about the history of the mountain and about some of the people who lived in the small farms they passed. Several times he had to get out of the wagon to guide the horses through ruts caused by streams of water racing down the mountain, but this didn't seem to bother him.

Near the top of the mountain, the steep, narrow trail conducted the travelers through canopies of oak trees and around sharp curves where they could have seen for miles if the mountain had not been surrounded by clouds.

"Over there is North Carolina," the driver called over the constant moan of the wind.

Laurel tried to make out forms in the valley below, but the white blanket of clouds only left her feeling anxious when the path led them close to the edge of the road.

Soon, however, the rain ceased, and the sun was trying to break through the clouds as the wagon passed by a bluff reaching high into the heavens.

"This looks like a good place for a photograph," the driver told the photographer as he pulled the horses to a stop.

"We can't get our photograph made," the lady with the hat complained, trying in vain to fuss and primp her wet clothes. "Not in this state."

"Look," the driver said. "The management told me to let this-here man get a picture to advertise the hotel, and I'm gonna follow directions."

The photographer carefully set his camera over his shoulder, and the travelers hiked the short distance to the bluff, where the picture was taken. Laurel, who had never had a photograph taken of her, found it fascinating and smiled, though she had heard it wasn't the fashion.

The clouds were already settling into the valleys when the wagon rounded a corner and took the weary passengers down a lane laced

Weary travelers pose on Roan High Bluff, near the Cloudland Hotel.
(Courtesy Jennifer Bauer Laughlin, from *Roan Mountain: A Passage of Time*,
Johnson City, Tenn.: The Overmountain Press, 1999)

with rhododendron, followed by the ten-mile fence surrounding the
famous three-story Cloudland Hotel. Constructed of balsam harvested from the mountain on which it stood, the building was located
on the Tennessee/North Carolina border and stood more than 6,200
feet above sea level. Several windows adorned its L-shaped structure,
with many of them open to let in the mountain breeze in the insect-
free altitude. Broad verandahs stretched the lengths of the south
and east sides, for the comfort of guests who wished to enjoy the
panorama of more than a hundred mountaintops.

A few buildings were nestled among some trees and underbrush,
and Laurel presumed they were for the horses and carriages. The

windswept lawn afforded various activities such as croquet and golf and laid out several paths for adventurous guests to follow. While the other travelers were merely glad for the end of the trip, Laurel's artistic mind absorbed the beauty of the majestic hotel rising above the sea of mountains.

Mrs. Sanders and her two children, Hannah and John, were already there. They were surprised to see Laurel when the wagon finally came to a stop at the front steps of the large establishment.

"Laurel, we didn't expect you to be on this wagon," the elegant Mrs. Sanders said when Laurel stepped onto the damp yet well-kept lawn. "Isn't it a grand thing you came the same day as the photographer? We've been anticipating him all afternoon, and I'm afraid the children are tiring of their fancy clothes."

At this remark, Laurel noticed that the guests and even the staff were indeed dressed in their finest. The photographer was setting up his camera near the corner of the hotel, and people were already taking a seat on the hillside, eager to be part of advertising the grand hotel in the clouds. Laurel looked down at her simple, small-town dress, which was quite damp from the eight-hour trip in the wet weather, and suddenly felt plain in comparison to her employer.

"Miss Laurel," said a small voice at her side. "Will you sit with us? Mother said she wants to stay on the porch, but we want to sit on the grass."

The eager child instantly made Laurel feel welcome despite her appearance, and she allowed herself to be led to a spot on the grass, near the front of the group.

Once the picture had been taken, Laurel was shown to the large bedroom she would be sharing with Hannah. It was well furnished, with two small beds, a dresser, and a washstand. Each piece of the cherry furniture gleamed with polish.

Laurel changed into dry clothes, then unpacked and placed her belongings into the dresser. She put her travel log on her pillow so she could later describe the wagon trip and photographs, then laid her artist's kit on the dresser. She fully planned to capture the beauty of the mountain, even if it took every spare moment. When her trunk was empty, Laurel slid it near her bed and sat at a window, gazing out at the North Carolina mountains. She heard a knock at the door.

"Miss Laurel, are you ready?" John called from the hallway. "We want to show you around."

Laurel opened the door and followed the two excited children down the hall and out into the sunshine. When she had taken the governess position, it was clearly stated that she was to be a constant companion as well as instructor to the children. Though she was weary from traveling, she enthusiastically went with them as they dragged her down several paths that had been carved into the mountain.

"This is the Rhododendron Park," John told her as he led her around masses of thick bushes bursting forth with red blossoms. "And over here is our hiding place."

Laurel was speechless as they climbed onto a flat rock and looked over the edge at the valleys below.

When the dinner bell rang, the children escorted Laurel to the

Guests pose in front of the newly built Cloudland Hotel.
(Courtesy the Archives of Appalachia)

Fields of rhododendron in bloom (Courtesy Harold Lingerfelt)

large dining room, which straddled the North Carolina/Tennessee border. A white line was painted down the length of its polished floor. The elegant dining table also had a line down its middle, with TENNESSEE written on one side and NORTH CAROLINA on the other. John insisted they sit on the Carolina side. Their meal consisted of fresh vegetables and meat purchased in town, and the diners were charmed by mountain music as well as popular songs of the day.

After she tucked the two exhausted children into bed and told them one of the stories the driver had shared about an area farm, Laurel took a small lantern and her travel log and slipped out and down the stairs to the wide porch. Her day had been full, and the mountain air relaxed her. The wind hummed through the trees, and the faint sound of music drifted up to her from the grand ballroom on the lower level of the hotel. She missed her family, yet she felt completely at home in the "land of the sky," just as the brochure had indicated she would.

The summer blossomed forth, and Laurel and her young charges fell into a daily routine. Each morning, Mrs. Sanders, quite at ease from her many allergies, basked in the sun on the wide verandah while Laurel took her two pupils into the classroom of nature. She showed them how the stream sustained life as it meandered down the mountainside, growing larger and quenching the thirst of plants, animals, and man. She taught them the different types of flowers, and together they identified trees and animal life native to the area.

The hotel's activities along with old-fashioned games that children play adequately filled their afternoons. Laurel even taught the children some mountain games she and her brother had made up at their grandfather's farm. It wasn't many days before the children from the hotel's kindergarten were playing the games with them.

Rainy days were more of a trial. The children would grow restless and bored with reading and quiet games indoors. But soon the sun would shine again above the mountaintops, and if a storm was still brewing in the valley, Laurel and the children were occasionally treated to a rainbow so high above the horizon that it would form a perfect circle.

One misty afternoon as Laurel effortlessly drew a patch of rhododendron that grew along a path, she told Hannah, "I've been drawing since I was a young girl—even younger than you."

She handed Hannah the drawing pad and watched as the girl turned page after page of nearly perfect sketches of flowers and trees, the result of years of practice.

"These are really pretty," Hannah said, and Laurel detected a glimmer of interest.

"I have a new drawing pad in our room. Do ya want it?" Laurel asked.

Hannah's eyes lit up in anticipation, and Laurel led her inside and gave her the small pad, which she had intended to fill with pictures for her sister.

"Take your time and draw what ya see and feel," she advised the young girl.

For the next several days Laurel watched Hannah fill the pages of the little book with flowers, mountaintops, and rough sketches of the large hotel. The more she drew, the more expressive her pictures became, and it wasn't hard to catch a twinkle in Hannah's eyes when she studied the purple horizon stretching above the surrounding mountains. Laurel decided that a drawing of Hannah, along with the story of how the little pad had changed the young girl's life, would be a much better gift for Jenny, who was quite sentimental.

The mountaintops began to cloak themselves in bright oranges, reds, and browns as Laurel helped John and Hannah pack for the long trip back to the lowlands.

"Will you come stay with us again next summer?" Hannah asked.

Laurel leafed through Hannah's drawing pad and tucked it into a small satchel. "I believe I will," she replied.

"Bring your drawings of the covered bridge. I'd love to see them."

Laurel helped the children carry their belongings to the waiting wagon and watched them leave before she slowly went back into the hotel. Mrs. Sanders had gratefully paid for Laurel to stay an extra week in a larger room with a fireplace. Though she looked forward to the luxury of a week to herself, she was sad to see the children go.

At first Laurel feared it would be difficult to fill her days without the business of games and lessons. But on the second day, she discovered that her freedom came as a refreshing change from a life of serving others, and she found herself strolling along the paths, locating rare flowers listed in the hotel's ledger. Her long blonde hair was allowed to hang freely as she studied each delicate petal and leaf of the Gray's lily, named after the famed botanist Asa Gray. She spent several hours adding them to a new drawing pad, and she even drew extra copies to mail to her aunt in North Carolina.

Each evening, Laurel relaxed in a copper bathtub, then snuggled in front of the fire with her favorite books. On the night before her scheduled departure down the mountain, she gladly accepted an invitation from a young married couple to join them at a dance in the ballroom.

Sea of mountains postcard, dated 1910

The lively music surrounded her when she descended the stairs and stepped onto the large, polished floor. She was flattered by the constant attention from several young men who desired to be near the Irish girl who spent her days drawing flowers with her hair flowing in the wind.

Laurel smiled when she later retired to her room to pack her belongings into her trunk. The summer had been refreshing and delightful. Her travel log was full of the interesting events of her stay at the grand hotel, and her drawing pads were filled with sketches of the mountain flora. She closed the trunk and then slipped down the stairs to the porch one more time to enjoy the cool mountain air.

A Stitch in Time

❧❧❧ ❧❧❧ ❧❧❧ ❧❧❧

Autumn 1895

A leaf caught Laurel's attention as it released its hold on the tree in her front yard and fluttered by her window. She laid aside the book she had been reading and carefully pulled an unfinished quilt from beneath the blankets in her closet. She had recently returned from another successful season as a governess on Roan Mountain, followed by a visit to her grandfather's farm. It was during this visit that she found the quilt in an old trunk. Her grandmother had started the quilt as a gift for Laurel's mother but had not had the strength to finish it.

Laurel unfolded the quilt and fingered a pastel-calico ring of petals. The delicate fabric, gleaned from baby blankets and old dresses that she and her siblings had worn, had been fashioned into a flower garden on a field of tan. Her grandfather had given her permission to take the quilt home to finish it, and Laurel planned to give it to her mother on her next birthday.

Laurel threaded a quilting needle with a strand of heavy thread. She listened to her mother, who was in the kitchen below quietly humming while she busily organized orders from Laurel's aunt in North Carolina. For several afternoons, Laurel had shut herself in her room and examined the small hexagons on the quilt, adding stitches to the areas that hadn't been finished. Her grandmother had been known far and wide for her smooth stitches, but as Laurel worked alongside them, she was able to tell when the feeble hands had begun to waver. How precious those stitches were, even though they were crooked and uneven.

"Laurel," her mother called. "Could ya run this order to your father at the mill? It's a perfect day to be in the fresh air. Perhaps you could take your drawing pad with ya."

The blue sky and changing leaves beckoned to her, and Laurel once again looked out her small window. Her mother was right—a refreshing walk was what she needed. She quickly finished stitching around a purple ring and hid the quilt away.

Laurel delivered the order to the mill, then followed the course of the river on her way back to town. Goldenrod graced the roadside with a flaxen hue and attracted insects from all around, and overhead the noisy squawks of geese resounded. Laurel passed the livery stable and open market before crossing the weathered covered bridge into the new part of town.

The bridge has definitely helped the town to stretch beyond its limits, she thought as she stepped into the growing neighborhood on the west side of the river. She remembered how she had feared for her beloved fields when she was young, but when the large gingerbread houses had appeared, she found she adored them as much as she had her flowers.

Laurel placed a small blanket near the Old Sycamore Tree and reached into her artist's kit for her pencils and pad. Her aunt had sold all of the pictures that Laurel had drawn on Roan Mountain and had ordered some more. Laurel remembered seeing an abandoned bird's nest in the tree's branches the last time she had walked to the train depot, and she thought it would make a good subject.

The tree, bathed in greens and oranges, was located just outside the bridge; and while Laurel experimented with her colors, she could hear schoolchildren shout to each other as they crossed the river.

"Tag! You're it!" a boy called out as he ran from the bridge.

Books and lunch pails soared through the air and landed on the ground as the rest of the boys gave chase. The girls, with their pixie faces framed in waves of curls, exited the bridge at a much slower, more dignified pace, elegantly congregating in little groups, sharing childish secrets.

A sudden sensation of restlessness filled Laurel's being, and she drew her attention from the carefree children back to the bird's nest. With the exception of the quilt and her drawings, she had found little direction in her life. Jenny and May were both in college, and though Laurel was proud of them and their plans for the future, she didn't think that was the course for her.

Laurel let out a sigh, then packed up her kit and stood to fold her blanket. What had started as a promising day in the fall sunshine had suddenly turned dismal. She slowly crossed the bridge and walked home.

That Sunday in church, Laurel quietly slipped into the family

Sycamore tree (Courtesy Guy Burleson)

Old Presbyterian church in Elizabethton

pew, next to William, and was surprised when Joseph sat down beside her. She had seen him often at the mill, still working for her father, but until this day she hadn't realized how attractive he had become. His once lanky body had developed into a broad frame, and when the congregation stood to sing, his deep voice rang strong and true. More than once, Laurel caught her mind straying from the service to the tall man next to her.

"Trust in the Lord with all thine heart; and lean not unto thine own understanding. In all thy ways acknowledge Him, and He shall direct thy paths." Laurel adjusted her skirts while listening to the sure voice of her pastor, who was quoting her favorite scripture, when she noticed Joseph's Bible. She could tell by its wear that it was read often; the cover was bent and the pages were wrinkled from constant handling.

As Joseph leafed through Proverbs, trying to locate the passage indicated, a few faded and limp flower petals fluttered to the floor. Laurel looked from the floor to the Bible, wondering how the yellow bits of flower had gotten there, until she felt Joseph's eyes on her face. She glanced up to see the hint of a smile and felt her cheeks color.

The petals had been hers long ago. They had been a part of the daisy chain she had foolishly linked across the opening of the covered bridge. Joseph must have kept and stored them in his Bible at her favorite passage.

She could hear a snicker to her right and, realizing her brother had watched the whole episode, everything became clear. William must have told the inquiring Joseph about her favorite verse, and Joseph must have shared the episode with the daisy chain. Laurel spent the rest of the service desperately trying to regain her composure and pay attention to her pastor's voice. When the last hymn was finally sung, Joseph reached down and picked up the petals he had kept for so long.

"I believe these belong to you," he said, gently placing them in Laurel's hand.

"You kept them all these years?"

"I couldn't bear to see 'em float down the river with the others," Joseph replied.

Laurel watched a slow smile cross his lips before she allowed herself to invite him to dinner.

"I would like that very much," he answered, and Laurel led the way down the small aisle, still cradling the delicate petals in the palm of her hand.

The next few weeks were a blur. Laurel spent her afternoons welcoming Joseph's visits and her nights earnestly quilting the sentimental gift. When Laurel's mother was finally able to open the present containing the quilt, the family watched her gently handle the gift and then lift moist eyes to her four grown children. The fabric that lay before her was precious, and the prayers she had prayed over her offspring when they had worn the little garments that had contributed to the quilt had indeed been answered.

Following the traditional musical feast, Joseph invited Laurel to take a walk, and the two soon found themselves at the entrance of the covered bridge. Laurel felt along the frame for the nail that had long ago been pounded into the doorway. She smiled when she found it.

"I knew," Joseph said, reaching for her hand, "when I watched ya link those flowers together I'd someday be walkin' ya across this bridge."

Laurel laughed at the memory of the chain lying in pieces throughout the bridge. In all reality she would have been disappointed if someone else had broken it. She had been attracted to the young man from the moment he had teased her about May's kittens, and now here he was, drawing her to himself.

"Will you allow me to walk ya over this bridge as my wife?" he asked, tenderly caressing her cheek.

Laurel lifted her eyes to see his face. The gentle look of the man standing before her had captured her heart, and she realized that the daisy-chain fad of long ago had worked. How May would laugh if she were to ever find out.

"Yes," she whispered.

Joseph placed a soft kiss on her lips, and they walked hand in hand across the bridge.

Laurel was blessed with a rare winter snow on her wedding day. Her snow-white dress was trimmed in red roses; Jenny and May were dressed in scarlet. Sprays of holly and ribbons adorned the church, and the whole event held an air of festivity. Her father, uncle, and grandfather charmed the wedding party with the music endeared to Laurel's heart, and Joseph even surprised her by playing an old dulcimer she remembered her grandfather had retired when she was little.

"I know how much you love music," her sentimental grandfather said as Laurel gently brushed at the tears flowing down his cheeks, "so my gift to you is a husband who can play."

Covered bridge laced with snow (Courtesy Harold Lingerfelt)

As the newlyweds stood receiving their guests at the back of the church, Laurel's mother handed her a small gift neatly wrapped in faded paper. Laurel, who had already moved her hope chest to the old house that Joseph planned to rent from her father, was surprised to see a set of pillowcases.

"Your grandmother made these for each of ya for your wedding day," her mother said, and Laurel traced the mountain flowers delicately embroidered throughout. "Her eyes were fading when she stitched these, so some of the colors aren't quite right."

Laurel looked down at the cases and noticed that a few of the leaves were orange and pink and the flowers were a mixture of colors. "They are absolutely perfect," she said.

Following a large celebration at her childhood home, Laurel's father drove her and Joseph through the covered bridge in his newly painted wagon. The bridge was topped with snow and decorated with a holly wreath.

When they reached the center of the bridge, Laurel's father

slowed the horses, and Laurel could hear some laughing and scrambling coming from above. Several young boys were hidden in the rafters, and as the wagon approached, rice sprinkled down on the couple. Laurel turned to Joseph and was not surprised to see a look of mischief in his eye, as if he had planned the whole thing.

Laurel's aunt from North Carolina had rented a small cabin as a wedding gift, and her father purchased tickets for the trip there. Joseph had never ridden the train, and Laurel couldn't wait for him to enjoy the ride up the mountain. She herself had never traveled over the top of the mountain and down the other side.

The wagon resumed its pace to the train station, and Laurel was reminded of her favorite Bible verse when they passed beneath the Old Sycamore Tree and its bird's nest. All her life, God had been preparing her for this day, for her new life as a wife, a homemaker, and perhaps someday a mother. And as she lifted her eyes to the nest and remembered the quilt that now lay on her mother's bed, she knew He would continue to be faithful to direct her life, to quilt it together stitch by stitch and row by row.

Seasons of Life

❧ ❧ ❧ ❧

Winter 1900

Laurel could hear Pearl as the child put her favorite doll into the wooden crib Joseph had given her for Christmas. She was singing as she played, and while Laurel tried to remember a time when the child was not singing, a small crash drew her attention from her older daughter to a dirty toddler and broken plant in the corner of the living room.

If Pearl was her songbird, then Anna had to be her monkey. The child was constantly into something, such a contrast to her mild-mannered sister, and it hadn't taken long for the young parents to discover that more discipline would be required with the little one.

When Joseph and Laurel had returned from their brief honeymoon across the mountains, the large house near the mill, which had been the childhood home of her father, welcomed them. The furniture that had been used by her father's family still remained, and Laurel delighted in decorating the rooms with simple curtains and homemade rugs she had stored in her hope chest.

The house sat quite close to the road, and its back door led to a fenced-in yard with a chicken coop in the far-right corner and a dog-house in the left. The river that Laurel had grown up with ran just on the other side of the fence, and its close proximity had a calming effect as it cascaded over smooth rocks on its way into town.

* * *

A sudden wave of nausea washed over her, and Laurel had to leave Anna and quickly run to the bucket in the corner. At first she had delighted in sharing the news of another addition to her young family, but as the pregnancy had progressed and she tried to keep up with Anna, her joy soon waned and exhaustion set in.

"They're almost done," Pearl called from the living room. Laurel looked out the window to the mill and watched Joseph, William, and her father clear leaves and debris from the wooden screen just above the waterwheel before they followed the path from the mill to her home.

"Come and set the table," Laurel said to Pearl, and then she put the overturned plant back in its holder and went back to her work in the kitchen. Since the day they had moved into the mill house, Laurel had insisted on providing the lunch meal; but as she worked over the frying chicken, her stomach began to lurch again and she wondered at the wisdom of her generosity.

A tiny yelp followed by a giggle from Anna prompted Laurel to rescue the girls' puppy from any danger. The front door opened and the three men came into the entryway.

"Hello, Anna!" William boomed, and he lifted the child into the air.

Anna squealed in delight. Laurel scooted the puppy into the back room and joined her family at the table. Then she remembered why she had volunteered to feed the three men—the meal always had an air of festivity. The men shared the activities of the morning, and Laurel thought about how it broke up the monotony of her day.

"You two girls wanna go out to the mill for a little bit?" Joseph later asked, reaching across the table to wipe mashed potatoes from Anna's chin. "You'll have to bundle up."

"Is it gonna snow?" Pearl asked with childlike excitement, already dreaming about sleds and mittens.

"I'm not so sure about that," Laurel's father said, "but I do think it's gonna be a mighty cold winter. Yesterday, I saw a bunny hitchin' a ride with a goose as it flew south."

Laughter surrounded the table as Pearl caught on to her grandfather's exaggeration.

But the winter was mild and left as gently as it had come. Soon Laurel and the girls could smell the faint scents of spring when they pulled their small wooden cart laden with sacks of flour into town.

"Listen to the robins," Laurel said.

"Where are they, Momma?" Pearl asked.

Laurel pointed to the dogwoods, blooming in pinks and whites. "When I was a little girl, I used to walk on this road all the time. Of course, a lot has changed since then," she said as they walked into the small town, which had certainly experienced growth. Phone lines now laced the road, and some old houses had been replaced with new ones. The livery stable that was part of Laurel's memory of her childhood had burnt down the year before. Though the farmer's market

"New Town" Elizabethton (Courtesy the City of Elizabethton)

remained, several shops had moved across the bridge, spilling into the fields that had once been the home of Laurel's adored wildflowers.

"Momma, can I go on ahead?" Pearl asked when they stepped into the bridge. "I think the kitty is waitin' for me."

"You can go, but wait at the end of the bridge," Laurel replied.

"I wanna see the kitty," Anna said.

She was talking about the ragged-looking cat that could always be found beneath the covered bridge. As far as anyone could tell, the cat did not have a home or family, so Pearl had taken it upon herself to claim him as her own, and he seemed to look forward to her visits. He would follow them around town, but whenever Pearl tried to coax him to go home with them, the cat would never cross the bridge. Pearl had tried to carry him across once, only to be scratched for her efforts, so she had to be content to visit once a week.

While Laurel walked with her children through town, she was secretly grateful for the cat's fear of bridges. She didn't see how she could handle a new baby, a puppy, a cat, and Anna all in the same house.

"That is the mangiest cat I've ever seen," Jenny later said while she and Laurel sat at Jenny's table and laughed at the cat. He sat just outside the screen door, grooming his tangled white fur.

"I know," Laurel replied. "But Pearl doesn't seem to think so." The two mothers laughed again, and the cat turned and gave them what appeared to be a look of contempt before he went back to his futile task.

Pearl and Timmy, Jenny's oldest child, ran into the kitchen. "Momma, can we go outside and play?" Pearl asked.

"Yes, but stay clear of the mud. We got some more errands to run."

"Show Pearl the new colt, Timmy," Jenny said.

"I wanna see the colt," Anna squealed from her place at the table.

"No, Anna, ya need to stay in here and help me and Aunt Jenny take care of Susan," Laurel said as Timmy led Pearl out into the yard.

"How are things goin' at the mill?" Jenny asked.

Laurel took a sip of her coffee and watched Anna peek at the small baby, who slept peacefully in the makeshift cradle in the corner of the kitchen.

"Everything's fine," Laurel replied. "Though I don't get out there as much as I used to. I need to do some good hard cleaning to the shelves and stuff, but I just don't feel up to it."

"Maybe after the baby's born," Jenny said, and she and Laurel laughed one more time.

Laurel finished her coffee and stood up. "Maybe I can get Joseph to trade jobs with me," she said. She slipped a small sweater on Anna. "You ready to go, Anna? We're gonna go get a licorice stick at the drugstore."

"You make sure that cat goes with ya," Jenny said, opening the screen door and giving the animal a slight shove with her toe.

"I was hopin' he'd stay here," Laurel lightly replied before she gave her sister a quick hug and called to Pearl.

Laurel led her daughters through town, and the shabby cat trailed along behind until they reached the bridge, where he once again slipped away, ignoring the persistent pleas of Pearl.

"Shoo, Buster," Laurel told the puppy as she pulled a chair to an open window and sat down. It was another hot summer day; heat waves shimmered about, and Laurel hoped for even a slight breeze to flow through her kitchen. "Pearl, come get this dog and lock him in the other room."

"Come on, Buster." Pearl dragged the puppy from the room by his collar and then returned with Anna. "I'm gonna take Anna outside, Momma."

"Keep an eye on her," Laurel said. Then she leaned her head on the windowsill—another rush of pain was overwhelming her. *Oh, why did I let Joseph go to town today?* she thought. She had known that once he left, her contractions would start; yet he had seemed so excited about the new pair of grindstones, she'd had to let him go.

"Momma," Pearl called from the back door. "Anna's playing with the chickens again."

Laurel gave a long sigh as she lifted her head from the sill. If she could hold on just a little longer, Joseph would be home and then everything would be all right. But it wasn't Joseph who rescued her this time—it was William, who came in with Anna in tow.

"Anna's been causin' quite a stir in the chicken house," he said, putting the child down. He went to the sink for a wet rag. "Well, anyways, I've been wantin' to come. Joseph told me to check on ya. . . ," he began, and one look at Laurel told him it was a good thing that he had. "You're not feeling good, are ya? Why didn't ya send Pearl out to the mill?"

"I was just waitin' for Joseph to get home," Laurel said, suddenly feeling quite foolish. Babies don't wait for daddies on errands.

"I'll take the girls to Mom's and get Joseph and the doc for ya," William said, and before Laurel knew it he was gone.

If Joseph had secretly wished for a boy, he was not disappointed when Laurel gave birth to twin boys that afternoon.

"They're a mite bit small," the doctor told Laurel from her bedside, "but they'll be all right. What are ya gonna name 'em?"

"Joseph and I talked about naming them Jonathan and James, after their grandpas."

"Good men, good names," he answered as he tucked the tiny babies into her arms. "Is your momma staying here tonight?"

"She has to take the girls to Jenny's, then she's comin' back."

"Good. Now you rest up, and I'll be back to check on ya."

Laurel watched the doctor leave her room, then she looked out the window at the late afternoon sky. Twins. She should have known by how different this pregnancy was from the other two, but she never imagined such a possibility. Now, how was she going to care for twins?

"You two were a bit of a surprise," she told the sleeping babies. With a calm assurance in her voice that she didn't feel in her heart, she said, "I don't know how we are going to do this, but we'll manage somehow."

The remainder of the summer season was unreasonably hot. The young mother spent her days adjusting to the constant care of the two babies and trying to keep up with Anna. At night she would fall exhausted into her bed, only to be awakened several times by a crying baby. The housework in which she had once taken pride remained undone. It was all she could do to keep the laundry washed and her children and husband fed. Had it not been for weekly visits from her mother, she knew she would have been forced to give in to hysteria.

"Are the boys asleep?" her mother asked one day when she found Laurel hanging diapers on the clothesline. The trees surrounding her yard were clothed in a spectrum of autumn colors, and the crisp air was seasoned with the aroma of decaying leaves.

"Yes, and Pearl is watchin' Anna," Laurel answered, quickly glancing toward the house. "I don't know what I'd do without her. She's been real helpful."

"I know this might be a hard time for ya, Laurel, but I can't help but envy ya a little," her mother said.

Laurel looked at her mother in surprise. How could she envy a messy old house full of noisy, demanding children? She, who had made parenting seem an easy task, had kept everything under control and in impeccable order. Laurel felt that her own life had been taken over by little people.

"My house seems so empty now," Laurel's mother continued. She handed Laurel a clothespin. "If I could turn back the hands of the clock, I'd spend more time playing with you kids on my hands and knees instead of scrubbing floors."

Laurel reached into the basket for one last diaper and remembered the distant look of pain on her mother's face on Jenny's wedding day. Her mother was right. The children would grow quickly, and, though the thought of a peaceful house was inviting, she knew she would miss them when they left home.

"Well," Laurel said with a laugh, "when ya come in for some coffee, you'll see that I haven't scrubbed any floors in a long time." She picked up the empty basket and led her mother into the house, promising herself she would try to enjoy her children for the short time they were hers.

The May Tide

May 21, 1901

"Rise and shine, sleepyheads," Laurel told the two boys, who lay sleeping in their crib. She lifted them one by one and set them on the floor. The smell of fresh-baked bread wafted to the small room, reminding her that she had been working in the kitchen. "Your nap time is over, and I baked ya some fresh bread."

She smiled as she watched the babies reach for each other and snuggle together on the woven rug in the center of the room. Her house was beginning to feel like a home now, filled with the constant sounds of children dressed in homespun garments, playing with their small wooden toys. Another long winter had come and gone, yet the growing twins had been able to captivate their sisters when they laughed and experimented with crawling and talking. As spring approached, Laurel could finally say her family had settled into a familiar routine.

Laurel was overwhelmed with a sense of satisfaction as she returned to her large kitchen. The twins followed along behind her on their hands and knees, and she was giving them each a small piece of the warm bread when Joseph came in.

"The river is kinda high this afternoon," he said, "so I'm gonna be a little late for supper."

Laurel nodded as he wandered over to her cupboard to inhale the aroma of the bread. It had been raining continuously since the day before, so she wasn't surprised by his words.

"Your father asked me to keep an eye on the raceway in case any debris heads toward the screen."

"Do we have anything to worry about?" Laurel asked. She knew the power of the river when the current became strong.

"Naw, I don't think so," he answered. "But keep an eye on the doghouse, will ya? You might need to move the pups if the water gets too close."

Laurel watched him leave with a slice of bread and then peered out the window and tried to focus on the wooden fence separating her yard from the river. She could see the mother dog calmly feeding her puppies, and the dog didn't seem too worried about the noisy current. That helped settle Laurel's fears.

It wasn't long, however, before she heard a loud banging on her front door. She opened it to find her father holding the reigns of one of his horses. As she stood in the doorway, wondering why the horse

Watauga River (Courtesy Guy Burleson)

didn't have a saddle, Joseph appeared around the house with an armful of puppies, shouting commands which at first Laurel couldn't understand.

"Get the children!" he cried again and again, and Laurel hurried to obey. At first she thought her father had been injured and Joseph didn't want them to see, but when she walked past her kitchen window to retrieve a crawling twin, she saw that the river had risen quite a bit and was quickly spilling into her yard.

"Pearl!" she screamed as she picked up the two boys and scrambled to look for Pearl and Anna. Her father caught up with her to take the twins from her arms, and she ran frantically through the large house until she found the girls playing in their room.

"The river is rising!" she said breathlessly while she lifted Anna into her arms and grabbed Pearl's hand. The little girl's face was bleached white as she followed her mother down the long stairs and out the front door.

Laurel's father and Joseph had already hitched the horses to the wagon, and William was throwing blankets into the back. Laurel ran out with the two frightened girls, and she was relieved to see her father standing nearby, waiting to hand her the twins once she had settled into the wagon. Joseph ordered the two girls to sit still as he placed them at Laurel's side. Even active Anna saw the stern look in his face and dared not disobey.

"Do we have time to—" Laurel began as she watched her father climb up onto his horse.

"No!" Joseph snapped. At first Laurel's feelings were hurt, but when she looked up the road to the mill, she saw that the waterwheel was nearly covered with water. Her father must have seen it too, because he immediately urged Joseph to head toward town.

The trip was more difficult than they had anticipated. The roads were quite muddy from the steady spring rain. The frantic horses made it hard for Joseph to lead them away from the mud. Several times the men had to climb out and lift and push the wagon to drier ground.

At first the girls were quiet, but soon the puppies began to push their way out of their burlap sack, and Pearl spoke for the first time since they had left the house. "What about Momma Dog and Buster?" she cried.

Laurel held the girl's hand and assured her that the dogs would follow their puppies. When she looked behind the wagon, she found that she was only partially right. The mother dog followed, but Buster was already running ahead of the horses and wagon, trying to coax Joseph to move a little faster.

When they reached town, Laurel was startled by the confusion that prevailed. A long line reached from the edge of the covered bridge to far down the road, as wagons and people waited to cross to higher ground. Townsfolk were being ushered from their homes only to run back to rescue a cherished keepsake or small animal.

Laurel let out a cry when she caught sight of her mother, who was clinging to the quilt she had given her. Laurel's father beckoned his wife to the side of the wagon. He reached down and lifted her effortlessly into the wagon with the others. By then they were a part of the growing line.

"I was so worried when the men started banging on our doors," she wept. "At first I went to the church, but someone came and said that both rivers were flooding and that we needed to get to the other side of the bridge. I thought for sure y'all wouldn't get out."

She laid the quilt over the two girls and reached to take the twins from Laurel. Tears ran down her cheeks. She hugged the squirming boys close and relayed how Jenny's husband, Tom, had been at the train depot when a telegraph from Roan Mountain had urgently reported that a "heap of water" was heading their way. He and a number of other men had come across the river, warning everyone on the east side of the impending flood, and then they had left to help several families to safety.

As they approached the covered bridge for their turn to cross, Laurel looked into the swirling waters. Trees, furniture, and other debris floated down toward them and piled against the upstream side of the bridge. Luckily, an opening remained in the middle of the debris, allowing the water to rush on through. The family stared in dismay as their doghouse bobbed in the water, carrying a chicken desperately clinging to its roof.

At their turn, Joseph cautiously led the horses up into the bridge, which still bore the NO TROTTING sign. The ride was smooth, and the horses were responsive despite the waters rushing beneath their feet. When they reached the center of the bridge, several people began shouting, telling them to hurry. They heard a large crack as a barn, washed from its foundation, slammed the side of the bridge. The horses panicked, but Joseph and William got them under control. Laurel huddled the two girls closer as the wagon raced through the bridge and onto higher ground.

Joseph kept the horses and wagon at a quick pace so he could be out of the way while some men ran into the bridge to assist an elderly couple carrying bundles of mementos to safety. Laurel wept in relief

Debris left by the May Tide on the Nolichuckey River

A former storefront rests hundreds of yards from its original foundation, testimony to the destruction of the May Tide. (Courtesy Michael Joslin)

when the barn broke up into pieces and drifted beneath the rafters of the bridge. The townspeople who were lined up on the other side of the river were once again able to cross.

"Your dad and I are gonna go upstream and see if anyone needs some help," Joseph said as he unhitched the horses at Jenny's house.

"You be careful," Laurel told him.

"I will," he replied.

After Joseph left, Laurel went inside and gladly accepted the dry clothes that Jenny handed to her.

"You just change into these and I'll take care of the children," Jenny said.

Laurel put on the clothes and was finally able to relax, until the puppies, whimpering for their mother, drew her attention back to the course of events that had brought her to Jenny's. She tried to imagine her freshly cleaned kitchen flooded with water. Tears came to her eyes when she thought about her grandmother's furniture and old photographs.

Covered bridge circa 1900

* * *

"A cloudburst came rushin' down the mountainside," Joseph told them that evening, "collectin' creeks along the way." He set his empty coffee mug down on Jenny's table. "The Watauga also flooded, and that's why the Doe came back into town. If it hadn't been for that telegraph message, lots of folks mighta got caught up in it."

Laurel reached for his cup and filled it with fresh coffee. "What about the house and the mill?" she asked.

"I'm not sure. Things look pretty bad out there," he said, running a weary hand over his brow. "Maybe I can go look tomorrow."

The next day, Joseph borrowed a boat and paddled up the river to their house, which was still standing. The mill and several other buildings, including Laurel's parents' house, had been washed away. After much discussion, the two families decided to live together in the old mill house and sell off the land in town.

Laurel sobbed as she and Joseph swept mud and water from their home. The furniture, rugs, and heirlooms that reminded her of her grandmother were ruined, and the clean-up job took several days.

In every situation, though, humor can be found. In the case of the

May Tide, it came in the form of the cat endeared to Pearl's heart. When Joseph returned from his boat ride around town, he told the family that the cat could be seen high up in a tree, hanging on for dear life. No one seemed to know why he had chosen that moment in time to move from higher ground and cross the bridge, only to be forced up a tree by the rising waters. Pearl always believed that he had come looking for her, and her family often laughed at her childlike insight. For a long time after, the townsfolk marveled at the scene, and the eastern side of the bridge acquired the name Cat Island.

Railroad tracks mangled by the May Tide, Doe River Gorge

Typhoid

Laurel hung her dish towel on the hook near the window and looked out at the shadows darkening as the sunlight receded for the day. It was getting late, but it wasn't bedtime. Pearl and Anna were in their new room, and the boys played with wooden blocks at her feet. Joseph worked long hours at his new job at the Empire Chair Company and wouldn't be home for quite a while, so Laurel planned to use the time to unpack more boxes.

A local family had decided to move immediately after the May Tide, and Joseph was able to purchase their house for a reasonable price. It was pretty small compared to the large mill house, but it was on the west side of the river. After enduring the destruction the floodwaters had brought, Laurel was grateful to be on higher ground.

She listened to the indecipherable chatter of the twins as she worked. Even though they were identical, they had different personalities, different mannerisms. James, older by only a few minutes, was verbal and outgoing; Jonathan was observant and content to suck his thumb. Yet, from the day they were born, the two had been inseparable. They shared toys, slept together, and even held hands. Laurel often wondered how they would act when they were older. Would they have different playmates? Go off to college? Court? Each day

Downtown Elizabethton (Courtesy the City of Elizabethton)

they seemed to revolve in their own world of togetherness, and the young mother was intrigued by it all.

A noise at the front door caused Laurel to look up from unpacking a box of dishes. Joseph, with his hat barely on and his work gloves gone, stumbled into the room. Laurel quickly left the small kitchen to help him to the couch.

"The boss said I looked terrible and sent me home early today," Joseph said while Laurel laid an afghan over his large frame. "He's sending the doctor over now."

"You just lay there, and I'll get ya some hot soup," Laurel said, then she scooped up the two boys, who had begun to climb all over their father. She hurried back to the kitchen and set them, howling, into the playpen.

"You two stay put. You can play with your daddy later," she instructed, ignoring their cries as she turned her attention to the large cookstove.

The doctor arrived shortly, and after giving Joseph a quick examination, he ushered Laurel into the kitchen to get away from

Pearl and Anna, who had wandered from their room. "Joseph has typhoid, Laurel," he said in a quiet voice. "If we get it under control, the infection may last only two or three weeks, but it's pretty serious. Will you be able to find someone to keep your children?"

Laurel nodded numbly and reached for the telephone hanging on the wall.

"Good. Give him plenty of liquids and cold sponge baths tonight, and that might relieve his fever. I'll be back in the morning," he said as he gathered his large black bag.

It wasn't until after he left that Laurel realized she hadn't told him about suspecting that she might again be pregnant. It was probably just as well, because he might have made her leave too, and then who would have taken care of Joseph?

The moon's rays were filtering through the cloudless night when Laurel's mother appeared in a flurry of activity. She filled several small suitcases while Laurel kissed the tear-streaked faces of her children.

"Momma will come visit ya tomorrow," she promised, lifting each child into her mother's wagon. "Daddy will be better soon, and then y'all can come back home." But even as she said the words, Laurel knew the dangers of the dreaded disease, which, following the flood, had claimed the lives of several in the small community. She had dared to hope that her family would be spared.

For the next several weeks, Laurel spent her days tending to her husband's needs and visiting the children. Her mother, who saw how weary she was, sat her down at her kitchen table with a cup of tea.

"If I'm guessin' right, Laurel, you need about as much rest as Joseph does with the child you're carrying," she said.

"I was hopin' no one would notice until after Joseph was better," Laurel replied.

"A mother somehow knows when her daughter is expecting." She smiled. "And I also know that you won't do the baby nor Joseph any good by wearin' yourself out. Stay home and get some sleep,

Laurel. Don't ya worry about the kids, they'll be all right."

Laurel gave one last argument. "The boys' first birthday is comin' up."

"When Joseph gets better, we'll celebrate their birthday. You wouldn't want him to miss it would ya?"

"No, you're right," Laurel conceded. "He has already mentioned it several times." She agreed to the arrangement, though she knew she would miss the children a great deal.

"The doctor told me I'm much better," Joseph said one late summer morning. Laurel sat at his bedside. The sunshine streamed through the window and shimmered on the wall, reminding Laurel how much they had missed during the season. "He said the children could come home."

Laurel was delighted by the news, and with tears in her eyes she once again hurried to the telephone to contact her mother.

The birthday celebration for the twins was the best ever given in the small family. The two boys wandered around on their chubby little legs, much to the delight of the adults.

But a few days following the joyous reunion, Laurel recognized the warning signs as soon as she went to get the boys from their naps. James leaped up and reached for his mother with outstretched arms, but Jonathan lay with his feverish head on the pillow and gave her a weak smile.

Once again the doctor brought his black bag to the small house, and once again the children went to stay with their grandmother, this time with the exception of Jonathan.

Laurel desperately tried every method and remedy she could to heal Jonathan. No amount of coaxing from the doctor or her family could entice her to leave his bedside, not even for a moment. For hours on end she caressed the face and tiny fingers of the child, who only occasionally stirred from his restless sleep. A constant prayer passed through her lips as she begged God to restore his health, yet he grew paler as each day passed.

"Momma," he said one day as he opened his light blue eyes.

Laurel reached forward and touched his lips, realizing she had listened to his first word.

"Momma is here, Jonathan," she whispered.

Jonathan smiled before his eyes drifted closed, and Laurel watched the child's thumb silently slip into his mouth for the last time.

A dark shadow settled over the household while the whole family mourned the loss of the boy. The grief of little James was the most heart-wrenching, as he wandered about the house, looking for his twin. Mirrors had to be hidden from his view following an episode with his own reflection in a small looking glass.

The weather was beautiful when the family wagon drew up to the small grave dug near her grandfather's farm, yet Laurel did not notice. Her eyes were firmly fastened on the coffin of her cherished Jonathan and remained so until it was lowered into the cold dark earth.

Images of Growth

Winter 1911

"Laurel, you have some visitors," her mother whispered before she lit the lamp on the bedside table.

The bedroom door opened slightly, and Laurel beckoned to several pairs of eyes peering into the room, where she lay holding the new infant.

"It's a boy," she told her children, who crowded near her bedside. "And his name is Jacob." For several minutes the siblings rejoiced over the baby boy, especially James, who had begun to feel quite outnumbered amongst his sisters.

"Hi, little Jacob," he said, presenting a small stuffed teddy bear made popular by President Theodore Roosevelt and his famous hunting trip. "I'm your big brother."

"Can I hold him?" Meg asked her father when he stepped into the room.

Laurel glanced up from the infant. Meg, the child she had been carrying when she lost Jonathan, was now nine years old. Her birth had softened the blow from Jonathan's death somewhat, and Laurel had always treasured her as a gift from the Lord.

"You'll all get your turn to hold him while your momma's gettin' better," Joseph answered, and he tenderly stroked Laurel's long,

Downtown building on Elk Avenue, Elizabethton (Courtesy Guy Burleson)

flowing hair, which fanned out on the pillow. "He looks so much like the twins when they were born."

Laurel nodded in agreement. She had thought the same thing, but she hadn't been sure how to mention it without painfully thinking of her baby who lay buried on the mountain. James, however, seemed pleased at the compliment, and Laurel was glad Joseph had spoken up.

"The snow keeps comin' down out there," Pearl said, gracefully moving from Laurel's bed to open the heavy curtains on the room's large windows. "Daddy says he might take us for a walk around town."

Laurel watched the young girl gaze out into the snow and she thought about her little town. The fields she had known as a child had developed into a bustling town with general stores, a bank, and even a newspaper.

Meg jumped up and down excitedly. "Maybe if we can find some nickels we can see a movin' picture at the nickelodeon. Do ya have any nickels, Momma?" Meg asked as she smoothed the peach-fuzz hair on Jacob's head.

"You silly goose," Anna fussed from the other side of the bed. "Momma is still in her nightie. How can she have any nickels?"

"I think I have some in my purse, Meg," the understanding grand-mother said. "Y'all come with me and leave your momma be." She gave Laurel a quick smile before ushering the small group out the door.

When they left, Joseph leaned over and gave Laurel a gentle kiss on her cheek. "I might even take 'em all sleddin' while you rest up," he said, and then he pulled an extra sweater from the dresser and quietly left the room.

Laurel looked out the window, where ice crystals had formed lacy designs on the glass. For a brief moment she longed to be outside with her children, walking around town and whisking down the hill on the cold hard snow. But the soft sounds of the baby at her side settled her desires, and she caressed him one more time and drifted off to sleep.

The following years were a treat for Laurel. Each day after school, the girls excitedly took turns tending to Jacob's needs, but his most faithful attendant was James. Laurel would never have thought a boy of thirteen would be so interested, yet he often lingered

Winter scene of the Doe River and the covered bridge
(Courtesy Johnny Holder)

nearby, speaking softly to the child.

"When ya grow up, I'm gonna tell ya all about your brother Jonathan," Laurel heard him tell Jacob one day. She had just dipped her hands into a sink full of hot, soapy dishwater and paused to hear what he would say next.

"He was just a little tyke like you, and, boy, did he like to play with blocks. Momma said he went home to Heaven to be with Jesus, and someday you and I'll get to go see him."

"Go see 'im," Jacob said, and Laurel let out a soft sob when the toddler lifted a chubby finger up to Heaven.

"Yes, we'll go see him, but not right now. Right now we're gonna play in my room. Ya wanna see my new boat?" James asked Jacob. James took the toddler's hand and led him into his bedroom.

Laurel reached a wet hand to her cheek to swipe at a sudden trail of tears, then chided herself when she had to get a dish towel to wipe away the suds.

"James, will ya stoke the fire?" Laurel asked the boy the next day. She sat on the sofa with a large box of stereographs in her lap.

"Sure," he replied.

"Look, Momma, it's a camel," Meg squealed, holding a wooden stereoscope in her right hand and dodging Jacob's reaching fingers with her left.

It had been a rainy afternoon, and Laurel, who had chosen to disregard loads of laundry, sat near the warm fire with her children. She leaned over Meg's shoulder to see the clear, three-dimensional image of the pyramids of Egypt that, until now, she had only read about. "It's amazing that something built so long ago still stands today," she said.

"I would love to go there," Meg replied, and Laurel had to agree before she turned her attention back to the box.

The collection James had borrowed from a friend depicted events as far back as the Civil War to as recent as the St. Louis World's Fair and the R. M. S. *Titanic*. From the comforts of their own home, Laurel and her children had been able to tour the globe as efficiently as the best "armchair travelers" in the world.

"Here's one of a woman sittin' on a rock—hey, that's Cloudland Hotel," James called from his position near the fireplace.

"Where?" Meg asked, and she scrambled to his side, giving little Jacob the opportunity to slip the camel picture into his mouth. "You're right."

"Look, Momma," James said. He adjusted the focus and passed the stereoscope to Laurel. "Did it look that nice when you went up there?"

"It was beautiful," Laurel said of the splendid hotel, which now lay forgotten at the top of Roan Mountain. "There was a bowlin' alley and a dance floor inside, and outside sweet-smellin' trees and flowers graced the mountainside."

"You mean the flowers in your pictures?" Meg asked, pointing to the drawings that hung on the walls.

"Yes. We spent hours drawing those pictures, and sometimes when we were bored, we climbed all the way up Roan High Knob and threw rocks over the cliff and listened till we heard 'em drop below."

This Keystone stereograph shows a young woman visiting the Cloudland Hotel. (Courtesy the Archives of Appalachia)

"No, no, Jacob," James said to the toddler, who had dropped the soggy camel stereograph and begun to dig in the large box. "Do ya think we might be able to see the hotel someday, Momma?" he asked as he pulled Jacob into his lap.

Laurel looked at the picture once again and wondered how such a secluded hotel had managed to capture the interest of a photography company in New York. "Maybe, someday," she said before she placed the picture back into the box.

"I'm leaving for Aunt Jenny's, Momma," Anna called from the front room.

"Do you have the muffins?" Laurel asked.

"Yes, and I think Bobby is catching something, so I'm taking some soup, too."

"Good. Tell your Aunt Jenny I'll come over tomorrow."

"All right."

The front door closed, and Laurel turned her attention back to the stereoscope and a picture of the Statue of Liberty. A dramatic sigh at the window caused her to look at her eldest daughter, who was longingly peering out into the rain.

"Do ya think he'll come out today?" Pearl asked no one in particular.

"You asked us that already," Meg retorted. She repositioned herself on the sofa with an image of an English countryside in her hand. "We don't care if he comes out again to see ya. He was just here last night."

"Meg!" Laurel quickly admonished. "I think Michael will come when he is finished with his studies, Pearl. Rain or shine."

"I hope so," Pearl said. She gave a quick glance toward her mother and then looked back through the window at the rain drizzling down.

She looks so beautiful and grown, Laurel thought, her eyes resting on the girl. She quickly looked away and slid the picture into the stereoscope. The image blurred as she realized her daughter would soon be yearning to marry the young college student and make a home of her own.

"The rain's stopped, James. Wanna go outside?" Meg asked. "We can play tag."

James quickly put the stereograph back in its box and sat Jacob down on the floor. "You stay here with Momma and Pearl, Jacob. I'll be back in a little bit."

Jacob cried when they left, but Pearl beckoned to him from the window, and soon the two were gazing out at the yard.

"Do ya wanna go out too, Jake?" Pearl asked him as she rumpled his blond hair. Laurel looked up from the box she was sorting through in time to see the little boy look at his older sister with big brown eyes and eagerly nod his head. "Then let's get your boots on."

Laurel watched out the window as Pearl and Jacob joined their siblings in a makeshift game of tag around the house, and her fears were settled.

Maybe. . . , she thought as she set the box of stereographs aside and moved to heat up a pan of cocoa on the electric stove in her kitchen. *Maybe Pearl is still a child at heart, and I can hold on to her just a little longer.*

A Bend in the River

Spring 1914

Pearl's eighteenth birthday dawned clear and bright, but Laurel's thoughts were clouded as she walked home from the drugstore with a small bag of candles in her hand.

"I think Michael is going to ask me to marry him, tomorrow," Pearl had told her the night before. "He has hinted around and

Elizabethton, The City of Power, early 1900s
(Courtesy the City of Elizabethton)

even told me about renting a house here in town."

Laurel sat down on a bench near the road, and her misty eyes rested on the calm river flowing beneath the bridge. She shouldn't have been surprised; the young man had finished his schooling and had been courting Pearl for quite some time. But Pearl's announcement had surprised her, and she hadn't known how to respond.

Joseph and I couldn't have chosen a better man, but I'm just not ready, Laurel thought, adjusting her position on the bench and allowing her gaze to follow the course of the river. The gentle current leisurely drifted around a bend, and though from where she sat she couldn't see it, Laurel knew it then flowed into the Watauga River, never again to be known as the Doe.

Laurel brushed a graying strand of hair away from her face and slowly acknowledged that like the river, she too was at a bend in her life. Her children were growing and would be leaving the home she and Joseph had faithfully provided. She had known from the start it would happen but could always say that it was off in the future, until now; for, starting with Pearl, she would soon be letting them all go.

A motorcar went by on its way to the covered bridge, and Laurel left the bench and resumed her walk along the dusty road beside the river. James had said that the automobile would someday replace the horse and wagon, and Laurel had laughed when he talked. But now, as she listened to the hum of the engine as the car drove over the wooden boards, she realized he had been right. She wondered how long the old bridge would be able to handle the weight of the new contraptions.

"I guess you and I are growing old together," Laurel quietly told the bridge as she lingered at its opening long after the vehicle had gone. The bridge was in poor shape. The foundation was still sturdy, but the roof needed replacing. The siding that had once been strong and true was now cracked and, in some places, had fallen off.

"Hurry, Momma, everyone is here!" Meg called to her from their front yard.

Doe River (Courtesy Guy Burleson)

Laurel left the bridge and walked the short distance to her house. Electric lights illuminated the front room, and the lively tunes of yesteryear had already set feet to dancing. Laurel put her nostalgia aside and was even able to laugh along with Joseph when James pulled out his small Brownie camera, interrupting the festivity several times so that everyone could pose for pictures. But at the end of the evening, Pearl and Michael announced their plans to marry, and Laurel suddenly felt herself age a number of years.

"It didn't seem that long ago when you was changin' diapers and kissin' away small injuries," Joseph whispered in her ear as they watched their eldest daughter walk with her fiancé toward the romantic bridge.

Laurel glanced at the man who stood at her side and knew he would understand her feelings, yet she chose to remain silent.

"I'm afraid for your grandfather's health," Laurel's mother told her the next day. Laurel was working in her rose garden, and her mother sat on a small bench close by. "He insists on stayin' on that mountain, but everyone could see at the party that he's not at all well."

Laurel clipped around a faded rose and sighed. Here was yet another bend in the river. She, too, had noticed how weak her grandfather had looked when he played Pearl's birthday song, but she hadn't wanted to admit it.

"Has he seen the doctor?" Laurel asked.

"I don't think so; ya know how he is with doctors!"

"Maybe he just needs to rest for a while," Laurel responded.

But her mother had a reason to worry. Within a week the family gathered together at the bedside of the very sick man, and soon after they attended his funeral.

"Grandpa and I talked the day before he died, and he wanted ya to know that ya can move up here when ya get married if ya want," Laurel told Pearl as the two sorted personal belongings and cleaned Laurel's grandfather's bedroom in the old farmhouse on the mountain. "That way Michael can work with the farmin' like he wants to, and y'all won't have to worry none about the rent."

"Thank ya, Momma. We were kinda worried about what we were gonna do," Pearl said.

"I know it's a little far from town, but it won't be too bad with Michael's motorcar," Laurel continued. "Maybe when we get it all cleaned up, we can move your hope chest up here."

Pearl hugged her mother and went back to cleaning the room with a new fervor. The ache in Laurel's heart was somewhat relieved when she envisioned her daughter raising a family in the large home.

"Momma, look at this," Anna called.

Laurel set aside her cleaning rag and followed Pearl into the large sitting room, where Meg and Anna were kneeling over a small box that sat near her grandfather's chair.

"I always wondered what Grandpa kept in this box," Laurel said, peering into the simple container.

Inside were several notebooks labeled with the names of his grand-children and great-grandchildren. Laurel carefully opened the one with her name to discover that the yellowing pages contained the lyrics of every birthday song that had been given to her throughout the years. As Laurel read each song that had been stored away in her memory as well as in the small book, Meg reached in and pulled out a set of books tied together with a ribbon.

"The twins' books," she said, and Laurel was surprised to see that Jonathan's book, which should have been empty for lack of birth-days, was as full as James's. She opened it and wiped away tears that ran down her cheek as she read the songs that her sentimental grand-father had written for her child, who would never hear them.

"I guess we need to get back to work," Laurel suddenly said, set-ting the book down and once again brushing at the tears on her face. But even as she said it, she knew the girls wouldn't listen. Laurel picked up the rag and left them reading their own special books near the fireplace. She stepped back into the large bedroom, and the old vase that stood on her grandmother's nightstand caught her eye. She carefully lifted it from its place of honor to dust it, when a small note fluttered to the floor.

Dear Laurel,

It has always been such a joy to watch you and your children blossom forth like the flowers on our mountain. Now it's time for you to take some of the mountain home with you. In the field behind the house there's a laurel bush with strong roots that can be transplanted. Take it home with you and fill your grand-mother's vase again.

With love,
Grandpa

Laurel and the girls easily found the plant her grandfather had mentioned. It had a bright blue ribbon tied at its base, and Laurel's

Doe River flowing by the grand Lynnwood Hotel
(Courtesy the City of Elizabethton)

heart softened as she imagined her grandfather, in his illness, choosing the fullest of all the laurel bushes in the area. It was bare now, but Laurel would have Joseph and James carefully dig around its roots. She would find a place in her yard where it could once again flourish.

"I can't believe this day has come," Laurel told Pearl as she watched her glance into the long mirror and adjust her veil with shivering fingers. "It seems as if it was just yesterday when I was holdin' your hand and walkin' ya across the bridge to Sunday school for the first time."

"I remember that day. You had to spank Anna for gettin' in the mud."

The two women laughed at the memory, and Pearl pulled on her long white gloves and reached for a spray of wildflowers.

"Here comes Daddy," Anna called from the doorway. "Are ya ready, Pearl?"

"I think so," Pearl answered, fanning her flush face with the flowers.

"Here, let me open a window," Laurel said. A slight breeze flowed in and teased at Pearl's veil. Along with the breeze came the soft gurgles of the river that passed through the town, and Laurel was once again reminded of the changing course of her life.

"Here is my bride," Joseph said, stepping into the small room. "I just saw Michael, and he's as nervous as a cat. We'd better hurry or he might just run out the back door."

"Daddy, don't tease," Anna said in response to the look of dismay on Pearl's face. "He's just teasing, Pearl."

"Well, if he does leave, maybe I can keep ya for a little longer," Joseph said, gently placing a kiss on Pearl's cheek before draping the veil down over her face. "You look as beautiful as your momma did on our wedding day."

"Thank you, Daddy. I love you both so much," Pearl said. The soft rustle of satin filled the room as she pulled a single daisy out of her bouquet and placed it in Laurel's hand.

Laurel gave Pearl a long hug and stood back to allow the bride to place her gloved hand through her father's arm. The persistent pang of loss thundered in Laurel's heart, yet one look at Pearl's radiant face caused her to smile as she watched her eldest daughter gather up her flowing gown and slip out the door.

War Heroes

Autumn 1917

"I don't wanna go, but I gotta," James told Laurel and Joseph as he closed his small suitcase and adjusted the leather strap. "When the war's over, I'm gonna go talk to Doc. Maybe I can get a job with him and save up some money for school."

"You just keep yourself safe, son, and don't ya worry none about school. We'll get ya through somehow," Joseph said, before he took the suitcase and left the room.

Laurel lagged behind and watched with a burdened heart as her tall son pulled on the olive green jacket of his uniform. He had such plans, her James. From the time he was a boy he had talked about becoming a doctor and finding cures for typhoid and other diseases, but his desires had been postponed by the war.

"Are ya gonna go fight the U-boats?" Jacob asked, bouncing up and down on James's bed.

"You betcha!" James said. "And when I get home, I'll tell ya about it while we finish puttin' the sides on your wagon. How's that sound?"

"Great! Bobby at school is real jealous that I got a big brother going off to war. All he's got is sisters."

"Well, you tell Bobby that I can be his big brother, too."

The distant whistle of the train prompted Laurel to step forward and hand James his hat.

"I guess ya'd better go if ya wanna make your train," she said.

"Are ya sure ya don't wanna go to the station, Momma?"

"And make a spectacle of myself in front of all those people? No, I'm gonna say my good-byes here," Laurel said. But as she dabbed at her eyes with her small handkerchief, she knew she wouldn't have been the only sobbing mother at the station. The war had drastically changed the community; even the mountains couldn't protect the families from its effects. Since the tragic sinking of the *Lusitania*, several of the young men had longed to fight, and, as much as they wanted to, their parents wouldn't stop them. "Now, don't ya forget to write. I'm not expectin' nothin' long and flowery. I just wanna hear from ya."

"You about ready, son?" Joseph asked from the doorway. "Pearl is saying good-bye to Michael downstairs." He turned to his wife. "I don't think she's handling this very well, Laurel."

James carefully placed his hat on his head, then took Laurel's hand and led her down the long flight of stairs. "Don't worry about me, Momma," he told her. "I'll be all right."

Laurel paused on the bottom step and watched Pearl tearfully cling to Michael at the front door. "Remember, James," Laurel said. "I'm gonna be lookin' for those letters."

"I know, Momma. I promise to write," James said, and then he lifted the small suitcase and followed Michael through the door.

For the next several months, James kept his promise by sending several picture postcards describing beautiful cities he had seen and people he had met, careful to omit the horrors of war.

Laurel and her children relished the letters as they willingly accepted the unwarranted intrusion of war into their lives. They enthusiastically took every opportunity to give aid to the war effort. Jacob tacked war-bond posters to his wagon and pulled it door-to-

Soldiers from Carter County dutifully joining the cause of World War I

door, collecting worn garments and blankets to send to the soldiers. Anna volunteered her time, helping the ladies in the community, and Meg was usually at her side as often as her studies would allow.

News soon came from Pearl that she was expecting her first child, and Laurel was able to persuade her to leave the large farmhouse and come live with them. The pregnancy went well, and Pearl gave birth to a healthy baby girl. She named the child Abigail. Her presence was a small light in the midst of a darkened time. But as the war raged on, James's letters grew scarce and then stopped altogether. Laurel began to worry about the well-being of her son.

"Momma," Jacob called as he and Meg came into the kitchen before school one day. "Teacher is leading another spelling bee to raise money for the Red Cross, and Meg said I'm a good enough speller to win. Can I be in it?"

Laurel was mending an old blanket, and she looked up from her sewing machine. "I suppose," she answered.

"Good. I got a list of words and I'm gonna go to school early and study," he said and started through the door.

"Wait," Laurel called out. She removed the blanket from under the machine's presser foot and folded it neatly into a large box. "Will you two run this box of blankets over to the hotel on your way to school? And tell Anna to bring home more sewing when she comes. I just have one last blanket to fix and I still have plenty of thread."

Jacob slid the paper into his coat pocket and picked up the box. "Sure," he said.

"I can do it, Jacob," Meg said. She gathered her books and lunch from the counter. "You go on and study."

"She'll be in the kitchen, canning some vegetables to send on tomorrow's train," Laurel told Meg while she held the kitchen door open for Jacob, who carried the heavy box to his unfinished wagon.

"Momma, can ya watch Abigail while I run over to the post office?" Pearl called from the guest room after the two had left. "I want to get today's paper and check for a letter from Michael."

Laurel watched Pearl enter the room with the blonde-haired child in her arms.

"Why don't ya walk her in the carriage?" Laurel asked. "It's gonna be a pretty day."

"No, I wanna go by myself," Pearl answered, and she placed the child in the wooden playpen and quickly left the room.

Laurel gave a quick glance at the small child, then picked up the last blanket and resumed her sewing.

"Your momma will be home soon," she said over the gentle purr of the machine. "Maybe she'll have a letter from Daddy."

Laurel's feet stopped pumping the heavy treadle, and her hands rested on the coarse wool of the blanket. She wondered what type of news Pearl would bring home. For several months, daily headlines announcing machine gun warfare, muddy trenches, and tanks unceasingly dominated the papers. The engagement of the American Army had indeed proven successful in the crusade against the exhausted Central Powers, at the cost of many lives.

Laurel quietly gave the sewing machine's crank a twist, set the needle to motion again, and finished the blanket. "She might even have a letter from Uncle James," she said, trying to sound hopeful. She laid the blanket on the table and peeked into the playpen. Abigail was busy stacking wooden blocks, so Laurel took up a basket of fabric that she needed to wind into bandages and headed into the front room.

"Momma, look at today's paper!" Pearl exclaimed, rushing through the front door. "It says Germany has signed the armistice and the war is over! Michael and James can come home!"

Tears of joy slipped from Laurel's eyes as she imagined holding her son in her arms once again. She set the small basket of bandages aside and hugged her eldest daughter close; together they pored over the announcement.

For days the town celebrated as trainloads of soldiers returned. Banners fluttered from every home, and brass bands assembled at the train depot. Michael was among the first to come home. He held Pearl and Abigail in his arms for several minutes, while Laurel and Joseph looked on.

"I'm glad Michael is safe," Joseph said to Pearl. The family stood in the front yard and watched Michael place a small suitcase in the trunk of his motorcar.

"Thank you, Daddy," Pearl replied.

Anna stepped forward and gave Pearl a kiss on the cheek. "It's been fun havin' ya here," she said quietly. "Almost like old times."

"When James gets home, you come back and we'll give 'em both a little welcome party," Meg called from the front porch.

Laurel brushed at tears and watched Pearl take Abigail from Jacob and climb into the front seat of the motorcar, beside Michael.

"Thank you for letting Abigail and me stay," she said and smiled. Laurel smiled in return and offered a small wave as the family drove away. She would see them again soon, and together with James they would celebrate the triumph of the nation.

But in a matter of days, Joseph and Laurel were weeping over the

Soldiers monument in downtown Elizabethton
(Courtesy Margaret Hyder Devault)

telegram informing them that James, who had been terribly sick with influenza, had finally succumbed to the disease, which had claimed several thousand lives during the war.

"How are we going to tell the kids?" Laurel asked Joseph while she pressed the small slip of paper to her lips.

"I don't know," Joseph quietly answered. "Jacob was here when the telegraph came. He may have already guessed."

Jacob was sanding his wagon out in the small shed when his parents found him. "He isn't coming back, is he?" he asked.

"I guess he couldn't fight the sickness," Laurel answered from the doorway. She wanted to sound strong and supportive, but inside she was heartsick. How could her valiant son make it through the war, only to be beaten down like this?

"He always told me he was going to go to Heaven to see Jonathan," Jacob said, "but I'm gonna miss him."

"We all are, son," Joseph replied, and he held the young boy close. Laurel quietly left the shed to locate Anna and Meg and phone Pearl.

Once again the earth was opened up, and Laurel clung to Joseph as James's large coffin was lowered next to the tiny grave of his twin. Never when the twins were babies and she had fretted over midnight feedings and childish messes would she have realized that in this way she would have to say good-bye to that which she cherished most.

Hoover Day

October 6, 1928

The sound of animated chatter was followed by a rapid knock on the door. Laurel opened the door to see her four grandchildren all decked out in their finest, ready for a day of excitement and festivities designed to welcome Mr. and Mrs. Herbert Hoover.

"Grandma, can we pick some roses from your garden?" asked seven-year-old Joey, Anna's oldest son. "Teacher says that when Mr. and Mrs. Hoover drive over the Watauga River Bridge we can throw flowers in front of their car."

Laurel immediately led them into her yard and reached for her pruning shears. Her roses were the pride of her garden, but the faces before her looked so eager she could not disappoint them.

"You know, your great-grandma helped me plant these roses the year before she died," she told them as she clipped liberally. "She always liked working in the garden."

"Momma was talkin' about her last night," Abigail said. "She was tellin' us all about the quilt ya made."

Laurel returned her shears to their place and wiped her hands on a rag. "I have that quilt packed away in the guest room," she said. "Next time ya come over, I'll show it to ya."

Joseph laughed as he watched the small entourage walk around

Children came from far and wide decked out in their finest to welcome Mr. and Mrs. Hoover. (Courtesy Margaret Jones)

to the front of the house, laden with the fragrant flowers. "Mr. and Mrs. Hoover better know what you're throwin'," he said as they all left to walk the short distance into town. "Your grandma never lets no one touch her roses."

Laurel smiled at him and turned her attention to the city streets, which were decorated in red, white, and blue bunting. "I don't think I've ever seen so many people at the same time," she said. The streets were overflowing with thousands of people. The Tweetsie Railroad and other railroad "specials" continued to deliver visitors from neighboring cities and states, and automobiles filled the streets. "I hope we can find Pearl and Anna."

"Momma said they'd meet us at the drugstore," Joey's little brother, Joel, said.

"Well, then, we'll go get 'em and head on over to the bridge," Joseph told the group.

The whistle announcing the arrival of another train sounded loud and clear. "Can we ride on a train?" Joel asked.

"We don't wanna ride a train today," Joseph answered. "All the fun is happening here, and everyone is comin' to see us. But, some-

Hoover Day, October 6, 1928 (Courtesy the City of Elizabethton)

day, I'll take ya on the train. We'll ride over to Johnson City and see a movin' picture."

As they waited at a newly installed traffic signal, which had caused much confusion for local drivers, Jacob caught up to them with a young, redheaded girl at his side.

"Momma, this is Ruth," he said, reaching toward the blushing girl and pulling her close to Laurel. "She lives up in Butler."

"Jacob's told me a lot about ya, Ruth. I'm glad ya could come celebrate with us today."

"I'm afraid my father's not excited about being here," Ruth replied with a laugh when they were finally able to cross the street and resume their walk toward the drugstore. "He's still trying to find a place to park his motorcar."

"There's Momma and Aunt Anna," Abigail called out. "Aunt Meg is with them, too."

"I thought you had to work today, Meg," Joseph said as the small group congregated on the sidewalk in front of the drugstore.

"I do in a little bit, but I wanted to buy the kids some candy first. Momma, do ya think I can use some of your roses for the centerpiece at the hotel? I think they'll be perfect for Mrs. Hoover's reception."

"It seems your momma's roses are the fashion of the day," Joseph said, much to Laurel's amusement.

"Grandma don't care if ya use all the roses, Aunt Meg," Abigail announced. "See, we got some too."

"I see that."

"Use as many as you'd like, Meg," Laurel said. "The frost is about to get 'em, anyways."

"Thank you, Momma," Meg said. She reached inside her purse for a small bag of mints and gave each child a piece. "Now y'all be sure to throw an extra rose to Mr. and Mrs. Hoover for me," she told them.

"We will," the children cried as they popped the candy into their mouths. They waved good-bye to Meg and continued their walk with Joseph and their mothers toward the bridge.

Meg closed the bag of candy and gave it to Laurel. "You can give 'em the rest later if ya want," she said.

"I hope ya get to see the parade."

"All I need to do is work on the flowers; the rest of the reception is ready," Meg said. "I should get a chance to watch from the porch."

A loud cheer went up from the crowd, and Laurel left Meg and caught up with her family as they assembled along the new metal bridge that spanned the Watauga River. A thunderous roar resounded as dynamite exploded in a nearby quarry, heralding the motorcade as it came to rest at the edge of the city. Speeches were given, and the presidential candidate was welcomed with a key to the city.

As the cars resumed their trip into town, the children threw their roses, giving their own special welcome, and waved to their Uncle William, who drove past in the Model T that he had polished and volunteered for the Hoovers' visit.

The rest of the day was spent in a whirl of activities. Airplanes

The American Bemberg plant was a major source of employment
in twentieth-century Elizabethton. (Courtesy the City of Elizabethton)

soared overhead while hawkers sold banners, hot dogs, and soda
pop, much to the delight of the youngsters. The town elaborately
entertained Mr. and Mrs. Hoover with tours of the prosperous man-
ufacturing plants, feasts in the ballroom at the elegant Lynnwood
Hotel, and a grand parade through town.

"Teacher told us to pay special attention to the floats in the parade,"
Laurel was told again and again by the children, who sat on a curb,
munching on hot dogs. "She said they would show a lot of history."

And indeed they did. A Cherokee war dance was followed by
covered wagons representing the myriad of settlers who had ventured
west over the North Carolina mountains. Peacemaking founding
fathers from the Watauga Association led the Overmountain Men,
who were dressed for victory, and companies of Civil War soldiers
marched side by side in their blues and grays.

"Grandma, look, here comes Daddy," Abigail called when the
young veterans of World War I marched past to the tune of "The
Stars and Stripes Forever." Cheers erupted as the crowd turned
patriotic, but Laurel had to look away. It was a grand company of
soldiers, yet it was without her beloved son James.

When the last float had passed, the crowd drifted into the large field at the foot of Lynn Mountain to hear the powerful speech intended to help boost Mr. Hoover into the presidency. Laurel found the address riveting, though her attention was diverted several times by the children at her side.

After hearing campaign promises and seeing much pomp and circumstance, the townsfolk and travelers danced into the night at the Lynnwood Hotel. Eventually the Bemberg factory's ten o'clock whistle pierced the cold night air, and the people boarded trains and other vehicles to return to their homes.

Traveling aboard the Tweetsie Railroad
(Photo from *Tweetsie: The Blue Ridge Stemwinder* by Julian Scheer and Elizabeth McD. Black. Johnson City, Tenn.: The Overmountain Press, 1991)

"Will Jacob be home soon?" Laurel asked Joseph from the living room sofa, where she sat pasting the small program advertising the day's events into the brown pages of a thick scrapbook.

"No, he asked me earlier if he could take Ruth home in the motorcar."

Laurel laid her book aside and glanced at Joseph, who sat across from her. "She's a nice girl," she said.

"Yep. With Jacob courtin' and Meg workin', it's gonna be a bit borin' round here," Joseph told her, before he stretched with an exaggerated yawn, gave her a quick kiss on the cheek, and climbed the stairs to their room.

Laurel laughed. She turned off the small lamp near the window and watched a car from another town cross over the covered bridge. Their small but growing city had gained recognition throughout the country, and its future looked full of promise. As she thought about her grandchildren tucked into their beds, perhaps with the taste of soda pop still on their lips and planes flying through their dreams, Laurel smiled into the darkness, not even able to fathom the misery that lay at the door of the nation.

The Great Depression

Autumn 1933

A gentle breeze drifted into town and through the open window, and Laurel cleared away vases of autumn flowers from the dining area of the grand Lynnwood Hotel.

What a lovely dinner, she thought, gazing out the window at the setting sun. The flowers she had picked from the gardens, along with a live band, had set the mood for romance, and Laurel could imagine young couples strolling hand in hand toward the covered bridge as dusk settled on the town and the new streetlights came on. She would have loved to linger in the early evening herself, but Joseph would soon be at home, expecting a hot meal, and Laurel had housework waiting there too, even though her house didn't need as much care now that her children were grown.

Laurel passed a weary hand over her brow. She reached into a service closet for her purse and gloves and then descended the steps of the hotel. The economic situation that had swiftly depressed the nation following the election of President Hoover was still a cause of uncertainty in the community, yet she and Joseph were happy. Their grandchildren were a constant source of joy and distraction. Joseph still had his job at the chair factory, and Laurel worked a few hours a day at the hotel.

Downtown Elizabethton
(Photo by James W. Bogart, courtesy the City of Elizabethton)

Laurel's mind was focused on her children and their offspring when she let herself through her front door and set her keys and purse on a small table. Pearl's daughters had a talent for drawing, and Laurel reveled in showing them the pictures she had drawn when she was a girl. They especially enjoyed the drawings of the town before it had grown over the river, and they tried to imagine it without the covered bridge.

Anna's youngsters were quite active, and Laurel couldn't help but laugh when Anna shared their daily antics. The memory of Anna as a young child had still not quite dimmed in her mind, despite the years that had passed.

"At times I just feel as if I want to scream," Anna often said, and Laurel was reminded of the similar discussion she had had with her own mother so many years ago. A dull ache filled her being as she realized how right her mother had been. Once her children had left to begin their own lives, she longed for the days of diapers and first steps, even though the workload was difficult and consuming at the time.

Meg and Jacob were starting off on their own, too. Meg had married a preacher named Christopher and was expecting her first child in the spring. Jacob, who had been able to rent a small house near the town of Butler, finally proposed to Ruth and a simple winter wedding was being planned.

Yes, despite her weariness and the condition of the nation, Laurel felt that times for her family were good, and it was in this mood that she sat down with Joseph that evening to a hot stew prepared with vegetables from her garden.

"I was up at Pearl and Michael's today to help them with their fence," Joseph said.

Laurel nodded. She knew that his plans following his shift at work included helping his son-in-law with the fence around the cow pasture.

"Pearl invited me in for coffee, and I couldn't help but notice how much weight she has lost. Why, she almost looks paper thin." He paused and reached for a hot corn muffin. "I wonder if they're havin' a harder time than they're lettin' on."

Laurel was surprised at the comment. She had visited the farm a few weeks before. Why hadn't she, herself, noticed the change in weight in her eldest daughter? *Yes, Pearl's mood had been melancholy,* she thought, *but hasn't she always been that way?*

"Maybe I'll go up there tomorrow," she said, offering Joseph another cup of coffee. "It's my day off."

"That sounds good. She'll be glad to see ya."

The next afternoon Pearl was quiet and withdrawn. She and Laurel hung worn and patched clothes on a line strung just outside the back door. She did indeed look thin. Pearl concentrated on smoothing wrinkles in a skirt before she draped it on the long rope. Her hands had always been long and slender, but Laurel was alarmed to see the bony quality of an elderly woman's hands rather than those of a youthful lady in her thirties.

The whistling of the teakettle summoned from inside, and Pearl excused herself. Overhead, a perfectly formed arrow of geese headed south, and a frigid autumn breeze whined through the branches of an oak tree, reminding Laurel that winter was on its way. She looked around the yard and spotted the girls, who ran and played, seemingly oblivious to the depression the nation had been enduring for the last four years. Laurel sat on a wooden swing and beckoned to them. In all her years as a grandmother, she had never considered herself to be the meddling type, but she couldn't resist asking just one question.

"Your momma said you and her baked up some potatoes for lunch today. How'd they come out?" she asked.

"We dug up those taters last summer," Abigail said. "But the bin in the root cellar is near empty, so Momma didn't eat none."

Lydia, who was sitting on the cold hard ground, suddenly looked away, and Laurel knew there was something the girl felt she had to share but didn't want to embarrass her parents.

"What is it, honey?" Laurel prompted.

"Momma always says she isn't hungry, but I know that she just doesn't want to eat so we can get enough. The coal bin's low too." She finished in such a small voice that Laurel had to get Abigail to repeat the humble words.

Laurel was ashamed. She had heard radio reports of unemployment around the nation, and the newspapers pictured soup lines and starving children, yet she had thought her family had been able to elude the onslaught of the depression. Upon further investigation she learned that Pearl and Michael's potato crop had not been a good one and that even their canned vegetables were getting low.

During the next few weeks, Laurel and Jacob devised a plan where Jacob would work in a nearby mill in exchange for grain, and Laurel would work longer hours at the hotel and purchase ingredients to use with the grain to bake breads and pies. At first Pearl tried to refuse when Jacob delivered the goods, but he begged her to accept by telling her that he was blessed to be of some use to his nieces. In the weeks that followed, Pearl steadily gained weight and was even able to look with eagerness to the birth of another child.

As for the coal, Laurel discovered that both Pearl's and Anna's bins were low. She and Joseph developed an idea that included the children. Each Saturday, they would take a walk along the railroad tracks, buckets in hand, and collect coal that had fallen from the trains. Joseph made a contest out of it to see who could gather the most coal, and at the end of the day the bounty was divided up evenly among the two families. It was never much, but it always seemed to be enough to sustain them throughout the week.

"Went up to the farm today to help Michael with that leaky roof," Joseph said one night. He leaned back on his pillow and watched Laurel run a soft-bristled brush through her long hair.

"Yeah?" she said, effortlessly twisting the long strands into a braid and fastening it securely before she turned from the mirror.

"I'd say that our Pearl has that healthy glow back in her cheeks."

"She sure does," Laurel said, her eyes glistening with tears.

Outside, the winter winds blew; the years of depression would linger on. But as Laurel draped her robe over a nearby chair and slipped beneath the heavy quilt, she could rest knowing that though her children and grandchildren weren't the best-dressed people in the country, they were warm and their hunger was satisfied.

Doe River and ET&WNC railroad running parallel up Roan Mountain
(Courtesy Guy Burleson)

No Place Like Home

Summer 1939

The houselights came up, Dorothy and Toto had been safely returned to their Kansas farm, and Joseph and Laurel were finally able to lead Jacob and Ruth's child, Douglas, through the narrow foyer of the grand Bonnie Kate Theatre. The Technicolor Wizard and Munchkins had definitely captured the attention of the youngster, which had been Laurel's intention from the beginning. He had sat next to her during the movie and had held her fingers so tight that she thought they would break.

At the drugstore, Laurel looked down at her grandson and watched him finish a dish of ice cream. His face was still as white as a sheet, and Laurel guessed that maybe the film had been too much for the little guy.

"Grandma, do ya think there's a real magical land somewhere?" Douglas asked.

"No, it was just a make-believe story," she told the child.

Douglas sighed in relief, and Laurel lifted him down from the stool and helped him with his coat.

"When will Mommy and Daddy come get me?" he asked.

Joseph paid the clerk, and Laurel led the way out to the sidewalk. "They'll be here in the morning," she said.

"I miss 'em, but I like stayin' with you."

Joseph and Laurel listened to the child's endless chatter as they walked down the lighted streets to the front door of their house.

"You wanna sleep in your daddy's old bedroom?" Joseph asked Douglas.

The boy's face lit up, and he shrugged out of his coat and threw it on the sofa.

"I thought so," Joseph laughed before the two went upstairs.

Laurel went into her kitchen; her mind drifted to her youngest son as she set a teakettle on the stove. She had noticed the anxious look on his face when he and Ruth left earlier to attend dinner at a friend's house in Butler. Jacob had said they planned to discuss the unofficial reports being made by the Tennessee Valley Authority about building an earthen dam to help control flooding and water levels on the Watauga River. Even though the project would be beneficial to the community as a whole, rumor had indicated that it meant the sacrifice of the small town of Butler, where Jacob had just recently purchased a house.

Laurel was sitting at her table with an untouched cup of tea when Joseph entered the kitchen.

"You gonna let it get cold?" he asked.

"I was just thinking about Jacob," Laurel replied. "Where's he gonna move his family if the town gets flooded?"

"Now don't go believin' a rumor." Joseph walked to the kitchen door and turned off the light illuminating the backyard. "Everyone is just talkin' about it right now. Ain't no sense in gettin' yourself worked up 'bout nothin'."

Laurel walked from the table and poured her lukewarm tea into the sink. She hoped with all her heart that Joseph was right, for her son's sake.

"Some say the rumors are true and a dam will be built down at Carden's Bluff," Jacob told them the next morning. "But nobody ain't doin' nothin', and I think it's just a lot of stories being passed around."

Ruth called to Douglas, and Laurel could see relief in her daughter-in-law's face that hadn't been there the night before.

"Daddy says the dam isn't needed," she said. "He says the river doesn't flood enough for the area to have to worry about it."

"I hope he's right, Ruth," Laurel said.

Ruth accepted a hug from Laurel and opened the front door. "By next summer, all the talk will be forgotten and we'll have ya all out to a picnic," Ruth said. "You can bring the kids on the train. It's a pretty ride."

"That would be nice," Laurel answered quickly. She watched the young family climb into their car and drive away.

The train whisked along the small track, and the sun shone brightly, causing Laurel to pull down the shade on her window. All around her were travelers out for a Sunday-afternoon ride, but as Laurel's eyes adjusted to the dim car, she realized that most of the passengers were her children and grandchildren.

"When I was Joey's age," she told her family with a bit of nostalgia in her voice, "I rode on a train all by myself all the way up the mountain."

"Be careful, old woman," Joseph called from the seat in front of her, "you're gettin' ready to let them all know how old we are if you start talkin' about that hotel that's been dead and gone since before they were born."

"Tell us about the hotel, Grandma," several voices called out. Laurel laughed and went into full detail about the "good ole days."

"Oh, I know that roads are bein' paved and the automobile's pretty popular, but there's nothing like a train ride," she finished when Butler's station came into view. "I imagine the train'll never be replaced."

As the train whistled before its arrival in the sleepy town, Laurel was once again reminded why Ruth and Jacob had settled there.

Downtown Butler (TVA photo courtesy Blair White)

The tree-lined streets, which were adorned with simple houses, shops, and businesses, beckoned to them as they disembarked from the train and walked around the town. Several folk whiling away the peaceful hours on their porches called a friendly *hello*, and Laurel felt welcome.

"Have ya heard anymore 'bout the dam?" Joseph later asked Jacob. They had just moved a large picnic table beneath a shade tree and were watching the children play near the river's edge.

"Nope, not really. Rumors are still flyin' around, but I think I might still get a few years outta this land before anything is done."

Joseph looked around at the fertile gardens fed by the cool water of the Watauga. "Looks like good soil," he said.

"Yep, should bring in a good crop," Jacob replied.

Laurel came out of the little house with a freshly starched and ironed tablecloth and laid it on the table. "Ruth, call me when it's time to harvest," she said as Ruth, Pearl, and Anna brought dishes

Young children played along the unpredictable Watauga River.

and bowls of salads, meats, and desserts from the house. "I might be gettin' a little old, but I can still help with the cannin'."

"I think I might take ya up on that, Momma," Ruth said. She quickly inspected the table before she called the rest of the family to eat. "You might even get to take some extra produce home with ya—I think Jacob got carried away with his plantin'."

"I just wanted to be sure we had enough," Jacob said. He sat down at the table and pulled Douglas to his side.

Ruth laughed. "Well, I'm thinkin' we might get to feed all the neighbors, too."

The mood of the afternoon was merry as the large family settled down with thankful hearts.

Good-bye, Little Town

Summer 1940

"Momma, are you awake? It's me, Jacob."

Laurel sat up suddenly when she heard the voice urgently calling to her in the middle of the night.

"Joseph, did ya hear that?" she asked.

Joseph awoke, and the two listened until the voice came again, causing them to slip out of bed and go down the stairs.

Jacob, holding Douglas in his arms, was standing at the front door with Ruth at his side.

"The river's floodin'," he said with a slight tremor in his voice.

Joseph ushered them in, and Laurel ran back up the stairs for towels and blankets.

When she was finally able to offer the young couple some hot coffee, she could hear Jacob talking quietly while Ruth slumped down in the corner of the sofa. The young mother looked anxious as she sat there staring off into the distance, and Laurel's heart went out to her.

"They started poundin' on our doors around eleven o'clock," Jacob said. "And all I could think of was to come here."

"You did the right thing, son," Laurel told him.

"Will the waters flood us here, Grandpa?" Douglas asked sleepily.

"No, Douglas, you're safe—Grandma's got her house on higher ground," Joseph replied.

The mood lightened, but Laurel couldn't help but feel sorry for Ruth, who barely acknowledged her steaming cup of coffee. The memories of the May Tide and the destruction it had brought seeped into Laurel's mind, and she tried in vain to think of something to say to comfort Ruth.

"In the mornin' I'll go see if there was any damage to the house," Jacob said.

"No, Jacob, don't go." Ruth spoke for the first time since they had arrived.

"I'll be all right; I just need to check it out."

"Then I'm going with ya."

"No one's gonna go anywhere till the floodin' goes down," Joseph said with a quick look at his son.

Ruth seemed to calm at once, and Laurel was able to lead her to the guest room.

When the family awakened the next morning, they heard reports of the water's fury from all over: railroad tracks displaced from their beds crippled the train, houses all along the river were washed from their foundations, and bridges were covered with debris.

"Rumors about the dam have increased," Jacob told them when they went out a few days later to clean the mud from their house. Jacob and Ruth's house had received little damage, but the crops had been ruined.

"It'll be a shame to lose such a pretty little town," Jacob continued. "The townsfolk have worked so hard to clean it up. But I won't be surprised if the government comes in and takes it away."

Laurel looked over at Ruth. She was scrubbing the kitchen floor while fighting the tears that threatened to spill as she contemplated having to leave the only place she had ever known.

In the end, Jacob had been right. Construction of the dam was

Butler before the Watauga Dam was built
(TVA photo courtesy Blair White)

approved by TVA the next year, and soon after, heavy trucks lumbered through Elizabethton on their way to Butler and the proposed site. Jacob and Joseph often took Douglas and the other grandchildren over to watch the dam progress, and Laurel would visit with Ruth and try to lift her spirits. But soon the high-water markers revealing the impending depth of the lake were placed in the center of town, and Laurel could only stand by helplessly as Ruth stored up hurt and anger in her heart.

The bombing of Pearl Harbor delayed construction plans on the new dam, however, as the Japanese ushered the United States into war. Families once again joined together to support the soldiers who set off to fight in faraway lands. Jobs that at one time had been scarce were plentiful since production was up to aid in the war effort, but product shortages and ration cards now dictated what the population could use and eat. Laurel's teenage grandchildren were soon swept up in the excitement of the fireside chats and the military fighter planes, but the older and wiser folk of the town knew that once again they would mourn as more young men were taken from them.

Just as in the Great War, the Allies were able to turn the tide, and the Axis Powers were defeated. The nation burst forth in joy as young and old alike celebrated the victory, and the soldiers were once again returned to their homes.

But the end of the war meant the continued construction of the dam, and the large trucks returned with their loads of work crews on their way to the river. Laurel worked silently at Ruth's side, packing her precious belongings, while Jacob and Joseph made the little house as sturdy as they could. The children watched as it was lifted from its foundation, loaded onto a large flatbed truck, and moved to its new location on nearby farmland.

The winter weather held a chill when Laurel and Joseph joined

Beautiful Watauga Lake
(From the Appalachian Photographic Archive Collection, Courtesy the Archives of Appalachia)

Jacob's family on a hill to watch the mighty Watauga River seep into the little town of Butler.

"Grandma," Douglas quietly said at her side. Laurel looked at the young man, who had grown quite a bit since the day she had taken him to see *The Wizard of Oz* years before. "Is Momma gonna be all right?"

Laurel could hear her daughter-in-law weeping in Jacob's arms as the water slowly spilled down Main Street, past the few remaining buildings and into what had once been the foundations of homes and businesses.

"I mean, we still have our house," Douglas was telling his grandmother, "and it's nice and safe on a mountain. We won't have to worry no more about floodin'."

Laurel took his hand and squeezed it hard, not knowing how to respond, and the two stood together while the peaceful town of Butler was laid to rest at the bottom of a lake.

A Fading Farewell

Spring 1969

"Are ya sure ya don't want me to get the car?" Anna asked her mother. "It's a long way back to the house."

Laurel shook her head and lifted her weary frame from the bench in the big circus tent. She slowly followed Anna out into the bright sun.

"No, that's all right," she answered. "I'll make it. But I do believe this is my last time walkin' to the circus."

Behind them the metallic tune of a calliope music machine rang out, reminding the community of the menagerie of death-defying stunts, exotic circus animals, and hilarious antics of brightly decorated clowns. Before them, Joseph waited at the covered bridge.

"Grandma, hurry up," one of their great-grandchildren called. "Grandpa is gonna tell us one of his stories."

"You tell your grandpa I'm walkin' just as fast as I can," Laurel told him as he hurried ahead, carrying a box of popcorn in one hand and a candied apple in the other.

"Daddy sure does seem to have a lot of energy," Anna said.

Laurel smiled and watched Joseph laugh heartily at a story told by one of their teenage great-grandchildren. All around him the younger children balanced and twirled around on make-believe tightropes and conquered imaginary lions beneath colorful circus posters tacked to the entrance of the bridge; Joseph danced along with them.

"That man is gonna outlive me yet," she said.

"It's about time ya caught up with me," Joseph called when Laurel stepped up to the entrance of the bridge. He turned to the children. "Now that your grandma's here, I can finish my story."

The acrobats and lion tamers temporarily abandoned their cotton candy dreams of running away to the circus and quickly gathered around Joseph.

"Your grandma had her heart set on catchin' me for a beau," he said with a twinkle in his eye. "And she started loopin' those flowers together just as fast as she could when she saw me comin'."

"Don't you be foolin' those kids," Laurel snapped. "You know that ain't how it happened."

But Joseph's wrinkled face eased into a teasing grin while he pointed to some black-eyed Susans that grew wild along the river's edge. Laurel soon found herself laughing as each of the children scrambled along the riverbank, picking flowers to bring back until their grandmother's hands were full.

The thrill of childhood continued to reign in the form of games of tag when the family entered Laurel's yard, but she found a bench near her rose garden and slowly eased into it.

"Dating today is done quite differently than when we were young," Joseph was saying to the older children who walked at his side. He sat down next to Laurel and added one more flower to her overflowing bouquet. "There ain't nothin' in modern-day sock hops, football games, soda parlors, and drive-in theatres that can compare to good old-fashioned courtin'."

Even though they didn't quite agree, the children seemed eager to hear the stories of old. Joseph winked at Laurel and then spent the remainder of the afternoon talking about church socials and sitting in a front parlor, trying to woo a girl under the watchful eyes of her parents.

* * *

"Tell me, Laurel, how's your garden?"

Laurel couldn't help but laugh at Joseph's question as she clicked off the television and stepped to his bedside. The nation had just propelled another rocket into space before their very eyes on the black-and-white television screen, and he was thinking about her flowers?

She slipped another pillow beneath his head and tucked the woven white blanket carefully about him. "It looks lovely," she said while she brushed a strand of gray hair from his forehead.

During the weeks following the circus, the whole family was amazed by how weak and worn down Joseph suddenly became. The children stopped by on their way home from dates or events in town and were always welcomed with open arms, but Laurel noticed that Joseph didn't seem to have the desire to do much more than sit and chat.

A visit to the doctor, followed by tests and treatments, confirmed the diagnosis of cancer. It wasn't long before Laurel was visiting Joseph in the hospital.

"We had a freeze last night," Laurel told him during one of those visits, "but I think the roses will survive."

"Next spring, you should plant a whole row of black-eyed Susans," Joseph said dreamily.

A nurse came into his room, pushing a cart of medications, and Laurel impatiently brushed at sudden tears before she gathered her purse and gloves. "I will and you'll love it," she promised. But as she planted a light kiss on his sunken cheek and left the room, she wondered at the truth of her words. He had said "next spring" as if he were going to be there to share it with her. Yet here she was, walking toward the quiet hum of the elevator, alone.

She had marveled at the hospital when it was first built, with its floors of facilities and staff who whispered through the halls in their crisp white uniforms. She and Joseph had spent countless hours there visiting sick friends and had even sat in the maternity ward, await-

Carter County Hospital, Elizabethton

ing the birth of great-grandchildren. But now she resented the hospital as she walked past the gift shop and out through the opened double glass doors.

It was true that, on Joseph's better days, the doctors had given her permission to bring a child. Joseph would summon the energy to pluck away at his aged dulcimer and teach a few songs to the eager fingers, lest the craft be lost. The children looked forward to "music lessons from Grandpa," but Laurel wished with her whole being that he could be home with her, enjoying the warm sunshine in the garden instead of dwindling away in a hospital bed.

She was at his side when he breathed his last. The expression he rested upon her face was not the look of pain she had grown so used to seeing in the last few months of his illness; rather, it was the familiar old teasing look. It was the look he'd had the day he tore her daisy chain to pieces.

His funeral was one of rejoicing, for he had planned it that way. The mountain music that could not be contained in the hearts of the people flowed forth freely as friends and relatives came to remember the man who had celebrated his life each day and had now gone to spend eternity with the Creator of music.

Black-eyed Susans

Tears streamed down the wrinkled paths of Laurel's cheeks as she silently grieved the loss of her lifelong partner and friend. When the service had ended and she had lain a spray of wildflowers on his grave, she smiled at the memories of a young man standing in the shadows of the bridge, holding bright yellow petals in his outstretched hand.

The Lifeline

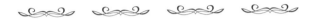

Spring 1976

The sound of young voices brought her back to the present. Laurel slowly lifted her body out of the old rocking chair and went to meet the children, who carried musical instruments and birthday gifts past a row of black-eyed Susans and up to her steps.

"Happy birthday, Grandma!" they called, and Laurel laughed as each child hugged her, nearly knocking her over.

"Now, who told ya it was my birthday?" she asked with a hint of teasing in her voice.

The children danced around her, and the next several hours were spent in celebration as her progeny rejoiced over the bounty of years that God had given her. The cherished mountain music she had grown old with once again filled her house.

After the cake had been eaten and the gifts laid aside, someone placed a small infant wearing a pink bow neatly tied around a wisp of hair into her wrinkled hands.

"I must be getting old, because I don't remember what ya named this child," Laurel innocently said, much to the delight of her audience.

"That's because we wanted to wait until your birthday to tell ya, Grandma," Benjamin, Meg's eldest son, said. "Her name's Laurel."

The covered bridge, soldiers monument, and Carter County Courthouse grace the edge of Elizabethton. (Courtesy Harold Lingerfelt)

Unbidden tears formed in Laurel's eyes. She beckoned to one of the youngsters who stood nearby.

"Go to Grandma's room and bring me the vase sittin' on my nightstand," she told him. "Be careful, it's very old."

When the child came back carrying the vase full of fragrant mountain laurel picked from the home's small garden, Laurel caressed the soft cheek of the infant still in her arms, then gave her back to her father.

"This vase once belonged to my grandmother, and I want your little one to have it," she told Jacob. The vase was set in a place of honor, near the faded drawing of the covered bridge on the little wicker stand.

"Momma," Jacob said, carefully guiding her down the steps of her porch. "We have one more surprise for you."

Laurel allowed herself to be settled into a wheelchair while the whole family, like a grand parade, headed down the sidewalk toward the covered bridge. Bicentennial flags and dogwood in full bloom laced the paved roadway; the scent of wild onions filled the air as a neighbor mowed his front yard.

"You know the bridge is going to reopen today," Pearl said when they stopped at the entrance of the structure, which was nearly a century old. "We thought maybe you'd like a chance to walk across it before the cars start driving through."

Laurel couldn't keep the shine from her eyes as she accepted help from several youngsters. She took slow, cautious steps into the dark opening of the bridge.

Beneath her feet she could see the calm water as it peacefully ebbed its way toward destinations she would never see. Passing the walls which had been eternally etched with signs of love, she watched mother ducks waddle through the park, calling to their young. The smell of fresh pine filled her senses.

"My daddy always said this bridge would help the town grow," she told the children at her side. She paused in the center of the bridge as a flood of emotions washed over her.

The mountain village of Elizabethton had indeed grown into quite a city, just as her father had predicted. The covered bridge that gracefully reached across the Doe River had provided the way for an

The Queen of the Doe
(Courtesy Johnny Holder)

abundance of families and businesses to come and settle, filling the old fields to overflowing.

But to Laurel, who stood while a cool, gentle breeze tenderly teased her silver hair, the antique bridge was a symbol of refuge, of true love, and of growth. It was a lifeline that spanned a century of memories.